# AGAINST THE GRAIN

*By Joan O'Hagan*

AGAINST THE GRAIN

DEATH AND A MADONNA

INCLINE AND FALL

# AGAINST THE GRAIN

JOAN O'HAGAN



PUBLISHED FOR THE CRIME CLUB BY
Doubleday
NEW YORK
1988

All of the characters in this book
are fictitious, and any resemblance
to actual persons, living or dead,
is purely coincidental.

Library of Congress Cataloging-in-Publication Data

O'Hagan, Joan.
Against the grain.

I. Title.
PR9619.3.038A7 1988 823 87-19509

ISBN 0-385-24319-7

Printed in the United States of America
*First Edition in the United States of America*

*for Jim, Noel, and Denise*

Whoever could make two ears of corn, or two blades of grass, to grow upon a spot of ground where only one grew before, would deserve better of mankind, and do more essential service to his country than the whole race of politicians put together.

JONATHAN SWIFT

# PART ONE

# THE SEEDS OF REVOLT

# CHAPTER ONE

AT THE RANGER URANIUM SITE in the Northern Territory of Australia, Robertson strode through the darkness. A middle-aged army captain, he had been seconded to take charge of security at this new mining site. His thoughts were still on a radio broadcast of a speech by the Prime Minister attempting to win more Australians to support lifting the ban on uranium mining. Heckling and loud protest from one anti-uranium group after another had been the Prime Minister's portion.

Robertson's lips curled ironically. Mine uranium? They'd mine it all right. No doubt of it. How many who heard that broadcast knew with what dogged energy the construction phase was being pushed ahead up here? Not those city types down in Sydney with their whining. The Government would lift Australia's four-year-old ban on exports of uranium. Up here they knew it. The snivelling environmentalists—goddam Parlour Pinks as they would have been called in Robertson's earlier years—they would be knocked back. As for the Aborigines and their protests about the loss of their land—much good they had ever made of it. The Abos would get money, more than they ever dreamed of.

Robertson often took a night shift on guard duty. He need not have done so, but he liked it, at night. It would be then that any attempt would be made. Threats had been made by anti-uranium extremists lately, threats to blow up the installations—machinery and construction work costing millions of dollars.

On the far side of the camp, from a checkpoint high in the mesh fence, he looked out on an affront to nature, shrouded now in night except for the perimeter illumination and a few arc lights—a great gash in the earth, piles of rubble, machinery, the beginnings of the yellow-cake mill. Robertson did not see it as an affront. It was mining to come. It was progress.

Under arc lights bulldozers were still at work moving earth, and trucks ground up the gully to the site of the new feeder road they were building to the Arnhem Highway. At the far end, and visible only from a height, was a small rectangle of green: the experimental crop looked after by old Charlie for the scientist fellow, Duquesne, who had, they said, gone back to Canberra.

Robertson thought suddenly of the journalist, Silkin, who was visiting the uranium site. Plying old Charlie with drink tonight, to make him talk about the wheat being raised inside the security area. Just what had Charlie told him before Robertson appeared? He had already caught Silkin nosing around near the wheat. Said he was sorry. Didn't know it was off limits. Silkin wouldn't be caught near it again, Robertson was sure of that. He remembered with pleasure Silkin's evident fright when Robertson's bulk backed him against the wire-mesh fence in a deserted corner. Much good his snob-school accent did him then.

Robertson swung himself down from the lookout and resumed his periodic check of the fence. The noise of the bulldozers grew less as he walked. At night the land was alive with animal and spirit presences that were sensed, not heard. Not only spirits. He caught sight of a pair of white eyeballs glittering in the moonlight, and a dark shape silently became absorbed into the surrounding darkness.

"Who's that?"

An Aborigine of course. Of course it could only be an Abo. The site was just within the Aboriginal reserve. No matter if a ten-foot fence surrounded the mining site. Abos—part of the land—could pass through anything.

Robertson completed the curve made by the fence at this point, and began on the long straight in front of Mount Brockman and the sacred Aboriginal site, going towards the experimental grain crop. Eucalyptus and wild quinine trees perfumed the air here. The grind of the bulldozers, which had faded, crescendoed.

Wait! Was that bulldozers? That vibrating, shattering roar?

You're imagining things, Robertson. The strain's telling. Six hundred men on the construction work, each of them immured for a three-month stretch. Orders were orders. And, by God, he would enforce them. . . . The bloody heat, the bloody flies, the bloody wet. . . .

It roared close over him, a juddering monster out of the north, bearing down, pausing; and then, descending vertically, it touched ground.

Robertson, transfixed for an instant, saw a quick flicker of light, which was an open door. A figure was briefly outlined, then disappeared; several hundred yards off a tiny light winked now here, now there, in the grain plot. All this, while the world still throbbed with the background roar of the bulldozers.

Why a helicopter? An attack. How many? What would they try to do? Robertson ran. And stopped suddenly. A man was scrambling frantically over the rough ground towards the helicopter. He carried something. He was no more than fifty yards from Robertson. His outline was clear in the part-lit night.

"Stop! D'you hear me? I order you! Halt!"

The running figure faltered, still a few yards from the helicopter, swung round. Robertson saw a white blob of a face.

"Stop, you bastard, or I'll shoot!"

Whether or not the man heard, with sudden decision he covered the short distance to the open door. He had a foot on the step when Robertson, cool now, brought his rifle up to his shoulder and snap-fired.

The helicopter, with renewed roar, was already leaving the ground. The runner's legs suddenly lost control; one leg groped fruitlessly in space for a hold.

Robertson fired again, then once more. The man on the step pirouetted in space, dropped like a stone. Gazing upwards, Robertson took careful aim and fired again, and again, until the magazine was empty. The monster, lurching clumsily, levelled off, an ugly awkward spinning top, completely blacked out now, and was lost to sight over the jagged outline of Mount Brockman.

In the gully, Robertson kneeled by the side of the fallen figure. He had fired at his legs, but one bullet had pumped a hole in the chest. The man was already dead. Robertson's torch played over a young blond-haired person wearing an anonymous outfit of drill slacks and shirt. Inside the shirt was stitched the label of a shop with branches all over Australia. The shirt was soaked in blood. There was nothing on him at all by way of identification. No wallet, no papers. His watch was a commonplace Seiko.

Breathing hard, Robertson stood up. The bulldozers, unheeding, ground away up the hill in the background. Sensing rather than hearing a presence, Robertson turned and backed a step. A figure came out of the darkness, and Charlie's voice sounded from it, cracked, panting for breath: "Christ!" He practically slid down the gully on to Robertson, who pushed him back roughly.

"Keep off."

"I saw it. He's dead. I saw you do it."

"No. You saw the helicopter."

"The blood." The old man was trembling. "He's only a boy."

"What you saw was the helicopter. You saw me shoot at the helicopter, but it got away just the same."

At that moment precisely, the bulldozers finished for the night, and quiet suddenly blanketed the area.

Robertson rounded on the smaller and older Charlie.

"Take his feet," he ordered.

The two of them staggered through the dark to the edge of the area being worked on by the bulldozers. Rarely imaginative, Robertson nevertheless saw them as gaunt prehistoric creatures savouring the few remaining hours of night. But his, his.

The men dropped the body, and Robertson climbed into the driving cab of the nearest machine. He expertly deepened for several yards the channel into which concrete would be poured the next day. The two men dragged the body to let it tumble into a queer position of prayer on the floor of dirt. It took Robertson no more than two or three minutes to rebuild the floor of the channel to its standard level. Nobody checked an odd few minutes of bulldozer activity. It was only a conscientious operator testing.

And that was all.

# CHAPTER TWO

In the house in Observatory Place, Washington, D.C., Temple had left his desk, as if by intuition, and appeared once more at the door. After some minutes Kohn said: "Oh God, no!" He lifted his head and looked to Temple.

"Art's dead. Dead. Miller had to leave him. They shot him." Surprise made his face look stupid.

"They shot him? The *Australians* shot him?" Temple's face, encased in fat, showed no emotion.

Kohn, adjusting his headphones, bent over the console suddenly. His pencil flew over his pad. Then he stopped and took off the headpiece. He was pale.

"Ten minutes ago Miller reported a hit in the fuel-tank. His gauge showed only a slight slow leak. He couldn't judge how serious it was, but he assumed the self-sealing would work. But then he suddenly came on the air: 'Losing height . . . engine missing.' They think he's crashed. He's gone dead."

Half an hour later a car door clicked shut out on the corner of Observatory Place and the man they knew as Colonel Chapman appeared. Into the frowsty regulated 72° warmth, he brought the crisp air of an April Washington day.

He said without ceremony: "He went down all right. In the sea. They've already salvaged what they could. The body . . ." His voice came to a stop. "There are a lot of sea-wasps around that coast. You die slowly, in agony." After a long pause he added: "Both boys showed courage, as we expect."

Temple was inspecting the window.

"They should never have lost their lives," he stated evenly.

"They were unlucky." Chapman's voice shook a little. "The bulldozing was to give them all the protective cover they needed. And they landed a mile from the actual camp."

"It's not a war. They had no right to risk it. And they shouldn't have been permitted to make use of the Navy like that, no matter how convenient."

"It was suggested—ordered, if you like. It was urgent."

"Why not leave it to the Navy, then?"

Chapman was angered.

"The last thing they wanted was to have an incident made out of it. It was a calculated risk, and it didn't come off."

"A calculated risk is one where the odds are heavily in favour of success." Temple's voice was coldly furious. "It wasn't so in this case."

Chapman looked curiously at him. It was not like Temple to become emotional. He said: "Do you want to tell it to the State Department? Anyway, there's no point in going over it again now." He paused and asked: "One of the boys was the son of a friend of yours, I believe?"

Temple nodded but did not respond otherwise to the question. "The Australians were well within their rights," he insisted. "Just as they were in their handling of Professor Nott. He provoked them needlessly."

"Oh, no. He only dropped behind the scientific team and shot some film."

"So they smashed his camera," said Temple with scorn.

"Yes," admitted Chapman. "He'd put it on a ledge while they were looking down on the excavations, and one of the Australians caught his foot in the strap. It went straight over into the machinery."

"What's his view on their trying to grow grain up there?" asked Temple.

"Trying to grow? You kidding? The stuff was stupendous, according to Nott. Satellite pictures just don't give a shadow of an idea of it."

"He . . . broached the subject, you said. What was their story?"

"Just a convenient spot to do some experiments on contamination from mining, once they get going. They said they're going to rotate a few crops and test them finally for air, water and soil contamination effects. They're worried about pollution of the Alligator rivers system after mining begins. At Rum Jungle, sixty-five miles south of Darwin, you can see miles and miles of dead trees."

"That may be so. But it doesn't make sense that a ten-foot fence put up to protect the Ranger uranium-mine site because of threats to blow up the installations should go a mile out of its way to take in an area of experimental crops."

"So we assume they put the crops inside a conveniently guarded spot because they want no unauthorised person to see them."

"Then their story about radiation testing is hogwash."

"I figure so."

"Isn't there another man on the job up there? Someone recruited in Australia?"

"Yes, a journalist. Silkin. We sent him up to Darwin to report on trade-union agitation against exporting uranium. The unions can make one hell of a lot of trouble. Then he heard about the grain crop. He wasn't able to get any plant material, though. But he gave us enough information about hours of work, bulldozing noise and so on for the helicopter stunt to be tried."

"I almost wonder", said Temple slowly, "whether it's the mining installations the Australians are so concerned about, or the grain crop."

Chapman said abruptly: "Bannister is going to be brought back from Australia. He hasn't been much use."

Temple laughed.

"Our bosses have finally worked that out? I notice Bannister never got up to those parts himself. He's competent enough where they talk American but not elsewhere."

Chapman gave the ghost of a grin. "The Top End isn't what most people regard as an ideal climate."

"The top what?"

"The Top End is what the locals call that portion of Australia. The Katherine-Darwin area, that is."

After a pause Temple asked: "Have they got someone in mind for the job?"

"Yes. You."

Temple was silent, in sheer surprise.

Chapman said: "You needn't feel awkward about it. Bannister

wants out anyway. You are at liberty to turn this down, by the way. Our boss is half-convinced that we'll never get anywhere with it. . . ."

"*Never's* a big word, Chapman," Temple said bleakly. "I'll be glad to try. With a better calculation of odds than those poor young bastards."

"Can you leave tomorrow morning?"

"My God!" Temple's feelings showed briefly behind the fleshy covering of his face. "Someone must know quite a lot over here to make it so urgent. Just where are we in this? Don't I get a briefing?"

Chapman said decisively: "It's the President's office, not State. There's a file here with full notes on the plant scientist concerned. I'll have the girl make a copy for you. Be very careful about making contact with the Embassy. We don't want the Australians to have any suspicion of you at all. Our Ambassador there goes along with us. He's a political appointee, thank God, so you won't have any trouble with him. Only he will know about you, but report to him only when it's safe and convenient. Forget about State Department."

Colonel Chapman smiled briefly as he added: "I'm told that the flies are as bad in Australia as the beer is good."

Later that evening, when all along Observatory Place suppers were under way, Colonel Chapman still sat at his desk dictating to his yellow-haired secretary, who sat patiently opposite, poised over her notebook.

"No words of mine," said Chapman, "can express the dismay and regret inspired in us all by the death of your brave son, Arthur.

"You will wish to know how he died. He met his death in a helicopter accident on a reconnaissance mission in South-East Asia. Security forbids me to mention just where.

"I am most deeply grieved that your boy's body will never receive the burial you would have wished. His body disappeared shortly after he was shot down.—No, don't put that in, Yvonne. Say: His body must forever remain in foreign parts.

"I can only assure you that no less than if he had died fighting a war did he lose his life in defence of the honour and glory of his country.—Delete 'honour and glory.' "

Colonel Chapman paused, considered, and said: "Type it out and let me see how it looks. Now take this down, Yvonne: Note for file, copy to Temple.

"Duquesne, John Edward: born 25 September 1940, Sydney, only son of Duquesne, Jozsef, Hungarian, doctor of medicine, emigrated to Australia 1937, and of Jane Mary Anthony, Australian, both now deceased.

"Educated Canberra High School.

"M.Sc., Sydney University 1961: D. Phil. (Cambridge) 1965.

"1966–70: Food and Agriculture Organisation, Rome. (Fieldwork in Indonesia, the Philippines and Sudan, on advisory activities in plant breeding and introduction, and related services.)

"1971–8: Senior plant scientist, Commonwealth Scientific and Industrial Research Organisation, Canberra. (Worked largely in the tropical north of Australia on pasture improvement.)

"1979 to present: Stationed in Canberra, CSIRO headquarters. Married. Wife Margaret Hill, born Sydney. Separated for several months from wife, who now resides Sydney. One daughter of thirteen, at present boarder at Bexley House School, Cremorne, Sydney.

"Interests: Underwater fishing (said to be an expert). First-class swimmer. Sports-car enthusiast.

"Owns house in Canberra and one on New South Wales coast (Rosedale, vicinity Batemans Bay) where he frequently visits.

"He is believed to be the scientist concerned with the grain which appears in satellite picture attached.

"Type out the list of articles and publications as well, Yvonne."

Colonel Chapman stared at Yvonne's retreating back. She was new and young, replacing his own girl who was away on leave. He wondered if he should perhaps have written that file note out by hand. But Yvonne had been thoroughly security-checked. She came back in record time with neatly typed pages. An extremely fast worker. The only mistake she had made this time was "serial" for "cereal" twice in a list of Duquesne's published titles.

Colonel Chapman stopped worrying. Yvonne was too stupid to be a security risk. He waited until the typing was finished, and Yvonne had left before he locked up.

Yvonne had tidied up her desk in her deliberate fashion, put on coat and scarf, left the deceptively ordinary-looking house, and was just in time to catch a bus down Wisconsin Avenue. Then she transferred and travelled as far as Rock Creek Park. She entered the park and, walking rapidly, reached a certain cluster of pin-oaks. When she was quite sure that she was unobserved, she dropped a pencil-thin cylinder into a cleft of one of the big trees, so updating earlier material on the Australian story. Then she continued her walk through the park.

# CHAPTER THREE

BY TURNING ON A LIGHT in his bedroom in the very early hours, Duquesne woke the birds with a false dawn. The whole of one side of the apartment consisted of sliding glass doors. These were the first sounds in the Canberra suburb of Hackett in the early morning: the thin inconsequent complaint of the magpies, inharmonious and disturbing, the occasional blackbird's rich fluty notes.

"Darling, do listen! The birds, too, are happy for us!" Irina had said, half-laughing, half-serious, as her hand explored his body gently. It had been at that same hour, a month ago, the first time they had slept together. Duquesne now thought gratefully of Irina, of her smooth firm body, of uncomplicated happiness. Already they were becoming dependent on each other, but Duquesne preferred not to examine what this implied.

For half an hour he read, until first one hand and then the other grew too cold. Then he luxuriated in the warmth of the electric blanket, watching dark shapes become furniture. It would be warmer in his Forrest house, old and solid, put up when builders took pride in their work. But filled with the history of his failed marriage, the mute appeal of the joint belongings of fourteen years, it was no place for him. When he had got back from the Top End this last time, he had advertised it for rent.

For a while he slept again and dreamed of wheat. Huge expanses of golden wheat. Sometimes it seemed to be growing in the inhospitable Top End, at other times in the vast areas of hungry Africa and Asia. Senegal and Sudan merged with India. Gleaming polished black of Africans became the slender dark intentness of Asia.

The common bond was his wheat. His miracle wheat. "Le Duc 1980" as he himself had named it.

He woke abruptly. In the sober cold light of dawn in Canberra,

Duquesne knew once more that he was finally near the stage when his almost unbelievable wheat discovery and its subsequent development could become a boon for a large part of the poor of mankind. It was an awesome thought and, had he been religious, he would have thanked God for the privilege of making this discovery.

It had been almost six years ago. Very early on a May morning he had gone out with Jackson, a government geologist at the Ranger uranium site in the Northern Territory. With them was Charlie, who had accompanied him on a visit to the Aboriginal wall paintings in the Nourlangie Caves. These were formalised recordings—older than anything in Europe—of events in the static everyday lives of prehistoric Aborigines, whose land was now being opened to uranium mining.

Charlie was pushing seventy. His life had been hard enough. First the war as a private soldier in North Africa and then in New Guinea, and then five hundred acres on the Daly under a War Service Lands Settlement assistance scheme—thirty-odd years of a grim struggle with flood and drought, crop failures, transport difficulties, disease and lack of capital. A heartbreaking repetition of the struggles of the early settlers of the region. A fighter as well as a self-taught but first-class agriculturist, Charlie had deserved better of life. Duquesne and he had become firm friends.

Duquesne had fallen behind the other two, and Charlie, turning back a little while afterwards, had found him on his knees among the high grass.

"I'm seeing things—it's the heat." Crouched there, Duquesne raised a pale face. "*Am* I seeing things?"

Charlie kneeled down, and Duquesne said: "Look! It's not the only one. There are dozens more."

The first ears were just escaping through the split in the sheath. It was a dwarf, and it was not free from disease, but the pustules on the leaves from rust infection, each surrounded by a halo of dead tissue, indicated an outstanding resistance to the spore infection. It had only a very few tillers. But there it was, a thriving specimen of *Triticum aestivum,* or common wheat, taking in water and minerals from that soil, taking in carbon dioxide from the air. A wild wheat—in those conditions!

"Wheat," said Duquesne in a reverent voice. "And already heading." He added: "It'll be ripe in a month."

"Surviving to this stage." Charlie spoke slowly. "With a high resistance to rust."

They looked around at the open woodland country, with its grasses already showing signs of the harsh drought.

In recent years, legumes of various kinds—Townsville stylo and also Siratro—had been distributed from the air in the area along with fertiliser. It was one of Duquesne's jobs to check on their response. If good, the area could support many more cattle. But this was different. This was wheat, a primitive wheat not known in Australia and with no affinity to the other grasses. Duquesne's hands groped and explored the topsoil.

"What's underneath?" he demanded of Jackson, when the geologist turned back to them.

"Round about here, of course, the soils are lateritic—the typical yellow podsol. With a concentration of radioactive minerals in them. Radioactivity up to five hundred counts a minute." Jackson grinned. "Good for mutations, eh?" He had just finished reading one of John Wyndham's classics of science fiction.

Instinct made Duquesne and Charlie keep the discovery quiet, each thrillingly aware of its implications, each unwilling for officialdom to intrude yet. Duquesne had surprised Jackson that night by getting uproarious on two glasses of beer. Charlie had been hardly less excited. The next morning, however, when they made off in their four-wheel-drive down the Arnhem Highway, twenty plants were aboard. From Darwin, Duquesne would fly the plants down to Katherine, and then take them to Charlie's farm on the Daly.

On the way, they talked and puzzled about the provenance of the plants and how long they had been growing there. Seed travelled by odd means. It could have been dropped by mistake together with the Townsville stylo seed ten years before, but this seemed next door to impossible. Such seed was carefully selected. The rogue wheat seeds would never have got into the mixture. Also, Duquesne knew the plants had taken very much more than that time to adapt to tropical conditions.

The seeding might go back a hundred or more years. Explorers, soldiers, fishermen, traders, settlers—all sorts had brought wheat to Australia. In the 1820s the first military settlers brought cattle with them to the Top End. Buffaloes had been introduced from the East Indies. Leichhardt himself, on his journey from Morton Bay to Port Essington, wrote in his journal of a valley which might have been the nearby Deaf Adder Creek. Had Leichhardt carried seed? Or had the wheat simply been accidentally dropped by some of those early settlers on the Daly or around Darwin? Remnants from the abandoned loads of failed expeditions, left to rot or to be plundered by Aborigines when frantic transients panicked in the hellish outback? They would never know.

But somehow the seed had arrived there. And then it had been subjected, possibly for tens of decades, to a high level of natural radioactivity from the rich uranium seam. Jackson had emphasised how, in that particular and limited area, the seam was almost on the surface, covered only by topsoil sufficient to sustain plant life.

At his farm, Charlie pointed out that attempts at developing an agriculture system in the whole area had a long history. He pulled out from under a pile of paperbacks and technical farming journals a 1960 report of the Department of Territories—the Forster report. It had told briefly—and not without drama—the story of agriculture in the Northern Territory, a story "remarkable in its alternating pattern of hope and despair." Even to the early explorers, the "land was either very good or very bad": for Matthew Flinders in 1803 "a poor dried up land afflicted by fever and flies"; but for John McDouall Stuart in 1862 "if settled . . . one of the finest colonies under the Crown, suitable for the growth of any and everything."

Wraiths from history rose from pages beginning to yellow—Maurice Holtze, in charge of the Botanic Gardens in Darwin for thirty-four years, saying in 1881:

"The following tropical plants may now be looked upon as a most perfect success:—Sugar, cotton, rice, maize, jute, tobacco, groundnut, sesame, indigo, grass-cloth, arrowroot."

But the pages were heavy with lost hopes. To this day agriculture in the Top End was no more than crops for fodder. Research and experimental work went no further than cattle breeding and pasture improvement.

So the Forster report had underlined how many attempts had been made, surely with plants and seeds from every other continent, to establish a viable agriculture. Somewhere along the mysterious path of history there had come to the Top End a wheat whose genetic constitution, when bombarded with high natural radiation, had brought about mutations enabling the plant to adapt to the harsh environment and to reseed itself there successfully. Under Mount Brockman, in the Ranger area, an unseen and undirected evolution had been accomplished. And it had been his, Duquesne's, role to lift the curtain on this work of nature.

In a specially constructed greenhouse on Charlie's farm, Duquesne had installed a growth cabinet to accelerate his back-crossing techniques under controlled conditions of sunlight, temperature and water. And he set to work to cross the Ranger wheat with the best types of wheat for yield and tillering potential. After painstaking trials, he had finally used NP 809, an Indian wheat already known for its high yield and quality. He had done what field-trials he could, and had even installed a miniature mill capable of testing the baking quality of his progeny lines. When—and only when—he had satisfied himself that he had actually accomplished the impossible—or so his conventional colleagues would think—and bred a truly tropical, eighty-day wheat, did he hand over his discovery to the Scientific and Industrial Research Organisation.

He then proposed to his chief that large-scale testing in Australia and in other countries be carried out and that the seed be sent to the International Centre for Maize and Wheat in Mexico. Something like a year had passed, during which one crop had been tried out under security at Ranger. Half-promises had been given him that other trials would be started in tropical Australia. Nothing had been done, nor had seed been sent to the world collection in Mexico.

Throughout the period Duquesne had worked to capacity, not only on his wheat, but also on a severe outbreak of disease in the rice on the sub-coastal plains. There was a stalemate on his wheat. In the Commonwealth Scientific and Industrial Research Organisation there was now a peculiar relaxation of effort, a reluctance to discuss plans or to make decisions. His chief, Beattie, had become strangely evasive; the chairman of the executive of CSIRO, Sir John Doughty, was never available.

By now Duquesne himself was even more keenly aware of the enormous potential of his wheat, its dizzying capacity to withstand drought even after the first half of the crop cycle had been one of tropical heat and wet, its promise—already in great part fulfilled—of high yield and general excellence. The sooner his wheat was thrown into the race for food production the better for the underdeveloped world. So long as it was withheld, Duquesne writhed in frustration.

There was one way, he thought grimly, to take the guts out of anything, and that was to treat it the least bit patronisingly and then leave it aside. Were they trying to kill it? He was ever conscious of the conventional attitudes of some of his nationally oriented colleagues, contrasted with his own feeling, developed during his United Nations years, for the needs of the poor countries.

Beattie, for instance, only the night before—with his direct frank gaze. One of Beattie's "heart to heart" talks. Beattie, carelessly lounging in his chair, one arm thrown over the back, had complimented Duquesne on his long, detailed report on the field-trials for Le Duc 1980, as his grain was now called. Again, Duquesne had proposed that the report should be submitted to the International Centre in Mexico.

"I know how you feel about Le Duc 1980. Indeed, I feel the same, and so does Sir John. We think, however, it's too early as yet to publicise a breakthrough like this."

Beattie had shifted in his chair, pushed it back, flung one foot on to the table, played with a glass paperweight.

"It's like this. We don't want to set something off we can't later control. It's a matter of . . . morals, almost." At this point he had laughed and given Duquesne an almost wry glance. "Think back to the late nineteen sixties and what happened in so many developing countries, like India and Pakistan and the Philippines. . . ."

"I should know," Duquesne had pointed out drily. "I spent most of 'sixty-nine in the Philippines on a field-job designed to iron out just such problems."

Beattie laughed heartily.

"Hell, yes! It had slipped my mind. Well, better than any of us you remember the . . . euphoria, you might say, which arose from the whole bag of new tricks those underdeveloped countries were suddenly presented with—the increased fertiliser, the improved methods of irrigation, the improved management, and the key of it all, the new high-yielding varieties of seed. Fine for the better farmers—the *better-off* farmers, who could afford it. Not so bloody good for the poor bastards who couldn't. The Green Revolution."

Beattie's voice had taken on a rhetorical sonorousness.

"I suppose the results were sufficient to justify the term 'Green Revolution' in popular usage," Duquesne said. "The increase of grain production in those countries was a solid fact. . . ."

"We scientists—especially nowadays—have always to see innovations in their broader setting."

Duquesne had said, with care: "I always thought we left that sort of thing to others, with intention; that any real breakthrough was ours to publicise—to the scientific world at least. And there our job began and ended."

"Come, not nowadays—not ever, at any time in the past, surely." Beattie, with the right shade and suggestion of vehemence, had surrounded Duquesne with words, and the pertinent remarks and questions contained in Duquesne's memorandum had been quietly shelved.

By six o'clock the light had filtered through the blinds, so Duquesne got up and made tea. Shaving in the little strip of a bathroom, his face looked back at him from the mirror—a thin boyish face with a wry twist to the lips, and blue eyes whose compelling depths his spectacles usually concealed. The eyes were also the eyes of his daughter, who was now—God save her—at boarding school in Sydney, because, his wife said, it was time she found her own feet.

But Duquesne did not want to think of his wife, whom indeed he pushed increasingly from his thoughts now. Restless, he dressed and made his way out of the apartment, directing his steps to Mount Majura, with its two humps, its long rough golden grass and the ancient ghostly army of its eucalypts, waiting and watching. From the nearer hump he looked down on Canberra sprawled flat in the basin, its lake gleaming coldly, ringed by brilliant blue hills. From the far hump he looked over the country stretching endlessly away, and he had the feeling, as so often came to him, that very easily could the sparse inhabitants who had come to this ancient country, together with their new cities and modern achievements, be swept away overnight without leaving a trace.

At the top of Mount Majura, Duquesne stopped and took from his wallet the personal memorandum hand-carried to him in confirmation of a telephone message the previous afternoon.

> Please proceed to West Gate, Prime Minister's Lodge, 3 p.m., Sunday, 20 April 1980, for a confidential meeting with the Prime Minister.

This could only mean that Australia would finally be undertaking full-scale development of his wheat. The hell with the cautious bureaucrats who had tried their best to stymie him. Duquesne laughed joyously, his brain racing ahead to the glorious future. Le Duc had made it, by God, Le Duc had made it.

# CHAPTER FOUR

"GET ME THE REPORT on the plant scientist."

James Blantyre, in the depths of his sanctum at Parliament House, raised his hard handsome face towards his secretary. James Blantyre, fifty-eight years old, third-generation descendant of an Australian shipping family, recent owner of a large wheat-growing property, Prime Minister of Australia.

When his secretary, Fisher, came back the Prime Minister said: "Read it out to me. Your résumé."

The Prime Minister sat with eyes closed, his head in his hands. Fisher knew that thus he would absorb every word. After he had listened to the details of Duquesne's professional career, the Prime Minister asked: "Why did he leave the Food and Agriculture Organisation?"

"He was offered a senior post here with CSIRO. His interests were always in tropical countries and in agricultural development, and his work here has taken him to the Top End for very long periods. He is now stationed in Canberra, of course."

"Married?"

"In 1965. A Sydney girl. They separated some months ago, and wife and daughter now live in Sydney."

"Why? Another woman?"

"No evidence of it. He is a quiet man, self-contained. Brilliant at his work, slightly erratic. A restless and enquiring mind. Staff complain that if he is on to something he will drive them without regard to working hours, but they are proud to work under him. Professionally strongly ambitious. His major interest outside work is underwater fishing."

"Politics?"

"Nothing there."

"Anything personal?"

"He drinks, so far as is known, in moderation only. He is well liked by colleagues, both men and women. The reason for his separation from his wife could be because he is too much married to his work. No suggestion of homosexual tendencies."

"All right, Alec."

The Prime Minister, alone, unlocked a filing cabinet and, extracting a folder, gave himself to its contents. It was a memorandum two months old and had been seen by only a most limited number of people.

TOP SECRET

Chairman of the Executive, CSIRO, to Prime Minister.

I have decided on the unusual step of addressing this summary memorandum as top secret for your eyes only. The following CSIRO development may not only constitute a major scientific event, but it also seems likely to have economic and political implications of the highest order. The assessment of this aspect transcends the competence of my organisation.

BACKGROUND: Wheat is a major crop in Australia. Large areas are highly dependent on wheat. It produces substantial export revenues. The long-term imports of wheat in many developing countries and in the communist bloc show trends strongly and inexorably upwards. Scientific improvements in wheat have benefited yields in traditional growing countries, but have neither extended significantly the areas where the crop can be cultivated nor raised yields in more marginal conditions. Thus, while the requirements for wheat of these countries increase year by year through population growth and because of the convenience of bread over other food grains, especially in urban life, their production of wheat lags far behind demand.

CSIRO DISCOVERY: A senior plant scientist of CSIRO, Dr. Jack Duquesne, identified six years ago in the Northern Territory a very limited number of untended wheat plants which had apparently made a successful self-adaptation to tropical conditions. The origin of the wheat is not known, nor the length of time it had been reseeding itself. The wheat was found, however, growing in the vicinity of the Ranger uranium site, and had presumably been subjected for decades to a high level of radioactivity—a fact likely to be relevant to this amazing adaptation to the harsh environment.

Dr. Duquesne discovered the wild plants early in May. They were then beginning to head. By early June they had come to full maturity. This wild wheat has therefore developed resistance to drought, because, though the plants took advantage of rains in March/April to germinate, they resisted the dry-season month of May in maturing. The plants had also developed a high resistance to rust.

A scientific assessment by Dr. Duquesne, typed in one copy by him, is in my personal possession. The essence of the report is that a fortuitous but true mutation or series of mutations took place, caused or assisted by strong natural environmental radiation from uranium seams in the area of growth. The mutation(s), transmitted through successive generations, has enabled the wheat plants to grow successfully in tropical conditions characterised by alternating periods of high rainfall and drought.

Dr. Duquesne has spent the last six years working intensively to produce through back-crossing a wheat plant which would combine the drought- and rust-resistant qualities of his wild wheat with the high yielding capacity and quality of other wheats. He has now produced Le Duc 1980 (technical report attached), which, according to the very limited testing possible up till now, promises to be an enormous step forward in wheat breeding. It is certainly far more promising than the fixation of nitrogen by cereals which is the major line of advance being attempted—so far unsuccessfully—in almost all countries.

The implications of the new wheat are therefore potentially so great that field-trials conducted by CSIRO have been restricted to a single crop, which was tried out inside the patrolled perimeter of the Ranger mine. Beyond myself and Dr. Duquesne, only three other senior staff members of my department, an army officer seconded to be in charge of security at Ranger, and the managing director of the mining company know of the trials. Others familiar with the area have been led to understand that

CSIRO are preparing to test the effect on common crops of local water polluted by the extraction of yellow cake.

IMPLICATIONS: Provided the provisional results are borne out, the area in Australia which could be sown to wheat would be significantly enlarged. We would also have a viable crop with which at least selected areas of the north could be settled, with all that this implies for the defence of this country.

The international implications are even greater. Wheat is one of the basic foods. In every developing country the demand for wheat grows faster than that for any of the other food grains. The Food and Agriculture Organisation of the United Nations projects that demand for cereals in developing countries will double by the year 2000—roughly twenty years ahead now—to the truly staggering total of 1 billion tons a year.

Now our new wheat introduces the likelihood that the poor countries, where natural agricultural conditions are frequently similar to those where this wheat was discovered, will be able to grow most if not all of the wheat that their increasing populations need. In doing so, they should be well on the way to solving their problems of hunger and poverty. There are obvious implications for wheat-exporting countries. Australian wheat exports could be expected to fall severely.

The adaptation of the plants to tropical conditions could also be cited as supporting the theory of the Russian biologist and agriculturist Trofim Lysenko, who denied the validity of the chromosome theory of heredity, and who maintained that heritable changes can be brought about in plants by environmental influences such as subjecting wheat to extremes of temperature. Lysenko's theory that, in accordance with the general ideas of Marxism and communism, acquired characters can be inherited is one which biologists have not yet disproved, though few subscribe to it. Apparent proof could again have political overtones.

CAUTION: This new strain of wheat has so far had limited field-testing. We do not know yet whether it is genetically stable, whether its success is dependent on some component of Northern Territory conditions which is not replicated elsewhere, how vulnerable it is to common disease, whether its grain will mill well on a scale bigger than has yet been tried, and so on. As a scientist, I must emphasise the necessity for thorough and prolonged testing of the strain in a variety of conditions before we can come to any firm conclusion as to its future.

OPTIONS: At this stage we have the option of

*(a)* releasing full information on the discovery and providing plant material for research institutes in other countries to undertake parallel testing, or

*(b)* restricting large-scale testing to Australia for at least another five years, in the meanwhile keeping news of our discovery and of our tests strictly to ourselves.

RECOMMENDATION: Despite the dangers of misunderstandings and the possibility of subsequent damage to the international image of Australia, as well as the implicit appearance of our support for the dubious Lysenko theory, I recommend the immediate release of full information on the breeding of this strain of wheat.

It will be obvious that secrecy would be difficult to maintain. Furthermore, Australia, which benefits from material received from CIMMYT (International Centre for Maize and Wheat Improvement) is under an obligation to make available to this institute its own new plant material, not least Le Duc 1980, which certainly promises to be *the biggest innovation in the recorded history of wheat.*

The Prime Minister was again struck by the fact that Sir John Doughty, whom he knew to be a cool and sceptical scientist of vast experience, had himself underlined the last nine words.

For some moments after rereading the memorandum, the Prime Minister sat staring at the opposite wall, utterly immobile, his mouth set in a hard line. His thoughts went back to his meeting with the American Ambassador in this very room two months before. With just the two of them present, the Prime Minister had talked of Australia's fear of nuclear proliferation and his government's intention to restrict sales of Australia's uranium to countries whose use of it would assuredly be for peaceful application. Australia was, moreover, very conscious of the desirability of keeping up American uranium supplies.

The Prime Minister had indicated the likelihood that his country, which contained at least a quarter of the world's reserves of uranium and a much higher proportion of reserves located in politically stable countries, would go ahead with uranium mining, conveying at the same time his anxieties about the strong opposition in Australia to this course. He had delicately underlined the desirability of long-term contracts as an insurance against the possible attempt at reversal of the decision to mine by a future Australian government of a different complexion. He had finally stressed his wish to compensate generously the Aborigines of the Northern Territory, should mining be undertaken. Their lives would undoubtedly be disrupted, and they would inevitably suffer the intrusion of undesirable elements into their traditional lands.

Their meeting had been bathed in the glow of mutual esteem and trust, which deepened at the end when the Prime Minister handed to the Ambassador a truncated copy of the CSIRO memorandum. Without the technical report. But only ten days ago the Prime Minister had acceded to the Ambassador's request, in the name of the President himself, for the technical report as well. No mention had been made by either side of the curious incident of the night visit of a helicopter to the Ranger area a few days before. Both knew of the incident. The American Ambassador was relieved that the Prime Minister could have no proof of the identity of the helicopter or its crew. He would have been impressed, had he known of the accuracy with which the Prime Minister's security staff had reconstructed what had happened. And neither knew of the delivery by a secretary of an additional carbon to a dropping point in Rock Creek Park, Washington, D.C.

# CHAPTER FIVE

The Prime Minister picked up the telephone and gave a curt order to Fisher. Twenty minutes later his Minister for Foreign Affairs, Sharp, and his Minister for Science, Turton, together with his Minister for Primary Industry, Bass, were seated on the other side of the Prime Minister's desk.

"Dynamite, isn't it?" Sharp was saying. He was small and dark and sardonic, and the Prime Minister thought that his eyes held a hint of disinterested amusement. "Manna to a food-hungry Third World, with all the glory that accrues to the giver. The Australian miracle wheat, backed up by Australian technical aid. And how Australia's image would be enhanced!" As well as the Prime Minister's own image, the eyes said, as a high-minded statesman with an enduring place in history.

There was a momentary silence, then Bass said thoughtfully: "The fact that we could grow wheat over a much larger range of conditions would probably be irrelevant because domestic consumption is changing little and of course many of our present buyers would no longer need wheat from Australia."

He glanced at the Prime Minister. In all their minds was the thought of Blantyre's own ten thousand acres and the "wheat" electorate which he represented.

"What did we export last year?" Sharp said casually. "Over six million tons of wheat? To China, India, Indonesia, Japan and Chile. Not the be-all and end-all of our exports, naturally, but of some significance—to the wheat-growers, at least. These exports wouldn't be needed."

"You have read the technical report, have you, Sharp?" interposed Turton. "The long-term usefulness of this discovery is quite unknown as yet."

"We must assume it to be a success, in order to make a decision," pointed out Sharp. "If we think it would be a failure, then there is no point in doing anything about it."

Turton began to speak, but Sharp brushed him aside.

"Demand for cereals in developing countries will rise to about one billion tons a year by the year 2000. A truly staggering figure, as the memorandum points out. These countries now have to import ever-increasing amounts from the granaries of the world, predominantly North America. We are all aware of the political clout which this gives the supplier."

"Even Australia," added Bass, "a relatively small supplier, exercises political influence in the Pacific basin through its wheat exports."

Sharp nodded and said: "It also seems, from the memorandum, that we would verify Soviet claims to have disproved conventional genetic theories."

"Leave Lysenko aside for the moment," growled the Prime Minister, who had already been lectured at length on the Russian's theories by Turton. He stared at Sharp, his mind busy with his own thoughts even while he listened.

"Of course, we can put a stopper to it," said Sharp in an almost offhand manner. "But if knowledge of what we have done leaks out, then we'll stink in every corner of the earth—at length and repeatedly—in a hundred international meetings."

"Now, 'stopper' is a word I'd prefer not to use." Turton, his heavy face comfortingly bland, was a positive antidote to Sharp's rapier-like quality. "The development must surely be exhaustively tested here in this country. It would be very wrong—morally wrong—and economically injudicious of Australia to divulge it before it is proved beyond doubt."

"Full testing can only take place outside Australia, can't it?" Sharp indolently cut through the speech that Turton was embarking upon. "If the discovery is stoppered—sorry, if it is exhaustively tested here—will CSIRO go along with this decision?"

"The man concerned," muttered the Prime Minister, "Duquesne, is raring to go. He wants to test it first in Nigeria, which has a general similarity of climate and conditions to the Top End. God knows where he'd go from there."

"The Australian tests have so far been extremely meagre." Turton spoke with great weight and gravity. "Surely there can be no real reason for hurry, every reason for giving due consideration to our position as—"

The Prime Minister, who had ceased to listen, began to speak quietly.

"You certainly realise that this is as grave a decision as we will ever be called on to make." He summarised the essentials with a clear economy. "We run a risk whatever we do. If we release details of the discovery now and the wheat proves successful, it is a magnificent feather in the Australian cap and the world benefits. If it isn't successful, our image as tough practical people is shattered. Equally, if we sit on the discovery while years of testing are carried out, eventually we'll be accused either of wasting time and money or, if it's successful, of callous disregard of the world's poor in favour of protecting our own exports. As our friend here says"—his eyes flickered sardonically to Sharp—"our name will stink throughout the world."

He paused and went on: "Release the news and we also rebuff our American allies, who want us to sit on the damn thing and who we know would be prepared to conclude a uranium-purchase contract that is unbelievably advantageous to us. They would, in addition, give enough money to make every Aborigine in the Northern Territory a part-millionaire. Then the lazy bastards could drink themselves to death in style, with plenty of whites to help them."

Sharp knew this was a reference to his family's large brewery interests, but he deemed it prudent to keep quiet.

The Prime Minister looked at the three men.

"Your advice, gentlemen, please," he said.

Sharp did not hesitate.

"Release details. By scientists. You should cool the thing down by a careful statement of qualifications. We'll have your statement in full in the *New York Times*, the London *Times* and the *Economist*, in *Le Monde* and so on. I think we could get *Time* to do a feature article. We're clean then."

"And the uranium contract with the U.S.?" asked the Prime Minister softly. "Just give away twenty years' contractual certainty of high prices and an assured market? Turton, what do you think?"

"Sit on it. Test slowly. Say nothing." Turton was shocked into uncharacteristic brevity.

"Bass?"

"For the sake of our own reputation, testing—full testing—should certainly be done first in Australia. There's rust. Now, rust itself mutates. The battle is never won there. It's a race to keep ahead of the constantly changing rust varieties. This wheat has developed resistance to types it would have been subjected to over fifty or one hundred years. What about those that might be encountered in the future?"

The Prime Minister sat immobile a long while and then motioned his three companions to stay seated. He picked up a phone and called Fisher into the room.

"Take this down, Alec." He dictated smoothly: "The Ministers for Foreign Affairs, Primary Industry and Science, having studied the report on a new strain of wheat evolved in the course of routine CSIRO research, advise that knowledge of this discovery be kept most strictly confidential until tests over an adequate number of years have been completed and have proved the viability of the plant in a wide range of soil and climatic conditions to be found in Australia and which can be taken as representative of conditions elsewhere. In proffering this advice, the Ministers have in mind only—no, delete 'only' —the long-term interests of countries which could exploit a fully tested and dependable plant innovation and the need for Australia to avoid arousing hopes which may not be realisable."

He stood up and said: "Get their signatures on this and then put it in my private papers."

Sharp thought swiftly. His position still suffered from the recent embarrassment of committing Australia in the United Nations General Assembly to the public backing of the wrong liberation movement in Africa. He had to recover before risking a confrontation with the Prime Minister.

"You may be right, Prime Minister," he said. "But I'm sure you would agree to adding in the appropriate place: 'The Ministers urge that testing be accelerated to the utmost degree possible.' "

The Prime Minister, who well knew the value of meaningless but face-saving phrases, said at once: "Of course you are completely right,

Sharp." He looked at Fisher. "Be sure you put that in. I'm going for a swim."

He grinned at them, a big strong handsome man, and added: "Where there are no sharks."

# CHAPTER SIX

FAR OUT along the Tharwa Road, Duquesne drove Irina's MG at a determinedly steady pace. She followed in his Alfa. With secret reluctance Duquesne had agreed to her driving it back from Timara Stables, where Irina worked. The Alfa was his darling. He loved its elegance of design, its precision and power, the cloth-ripping roar of its acceleration.

The Alfa snaked past suddenly, Irina's long blonde hair flying as she leaned out, shouting something, before she accelerated away. Duquesne understood. At just this point on the road they had met for the first time, over a month before, when she was caught with a flat tyre and a spare whose valve was missing.

Touching 150 k.p.h. now, she drifted around a bend and disappeared. Apprehension fought with Duquesne's admiration. She drove a car as she rode a horse—with the coolness of the professional, with the fire and *élan* of the artist. He had seen her that morning on a big black which she said was an ex-racehorse. He could believe it. Going hell for leather, a united pair—the black all mettle and breeding, Irina all fearless joy—aristocrats both. Irina's hair clubbed up beneath a cap, her handsome face intent, her green eyes glittering with excitement.

No wonder Vasily Sanin was—so far as Duquesne could make out—a frequent companion. Vasily, too, was an expert horseman, a big blond man, beautifully turned out. He had bowed and said "Pleased" when introduced, his gaze remaining just a fraction too long on Duquesne's old corduroy trousers and jacket. They had galloped through a landscape vivid and glowing, the cream paddocks rolling in velvet swathes to the bright quivering blue of the mountains.

Pausing in the rough foothills of Mount Tennant, Vasily had said:

"What a country for the sport, as easy to indulge in as all else! Marvellous. Australia Felix. The country without problems."

Like Irina, he seemed exhilarated by the gallop.

Duquesne said morosely: "There are one or two problems left."

"Ah, yes, by all means. The lack of them is problem enough. What I notice"—Vasily had smiled with complacence—"is few people, and people who do what they wish. Their liberty they have accomplished, and I suspect they seek meaning for their lives."

Duquesne stared at him in amazement.

"No doubt you could suggest something for us," he drawled rudely. "I can see you've done your homework." And, touching his horse with his heel, he jogged off by himself.

Back at Timara, Vasily had handed Irina down from her horse with ceremony, his hand lingering on her back as they chatted. She was wearing Duquesne's sweater, his red sweater that he had loaned her the first day of their meeting. It went well with her fawn riding breeches. She was always intending to return it to him, but never did. It was one of their private jokes.

Now they were in a hurry to get to Duquesne's house in Forrest, to meet a prospective tenant. But were they in this much of a hurry? Speed, and the concentration needed to keep it up, wiped out thought anyway. Was that why Irina . . . that feverish gaiety of hers, at times . . . ?

When they drew up outside his Forrest house, he was sweating. The Alfa purred as Irina drew demurely to a stop. She got out and swaggered a little—in slacks now—as slim and boyish as Duquesne himself, and as tall.

"Gorgeous she is, to drive." Her laugh was elation itself.

The prospective tenant arrived hard on their heels. He was tall and bulky with pale blue eyes and ginger hair. He walked up the path with the deliberation and lack of elasticity of the overpadded, moving all of a piece.

"Not even the cabby knew your street. He had to ask two people. You keep going in circles. The place is a maze." The voice belonged unmistakably to the Eastern States of America. "How do you folk ever find each other?"

"We don't always, and we blame an American called Walter Burley Griffin."

"Oh, yes, I know about him. They might have told him to go and get lost before they awarded him first prize for the winning design of Canberra."

The newcomer rumbled with laughter and shook hands. He said his name was Temple. His words dropped from him so indistinctly, almost grudgingly, that Duquesne could not be quite sure. He greeted Irina with attention, even gallantry. While Duquesne showed him the house, Irina disappeared.

In the kitchen Temple paused to cogitate. Rummaging in a pocket, he brought out a crumpled paper.

"M'wife's given me a list of things to ask. She's particular about kitchens. Let's see. The freezer is on the small side. No broiler. OK so far. Ah, dishwasher. No dishwasher, no garbage-disposal unit."

"You don't usually get them in a rented house here."

"The dishwasher is important. M'wife suffers from rheumatism in her hands. You like to install one for us?"

Duquesne considered.

"Yes, I could do that. There's space for it. The disposal unit, no."

"I'll take the dishwasher without the disposal unit. But you folk seem to like to make life a little unnecessarily difficult for yourselves. No central heating!" Burdened by fat, Temple's pale eyes looked out at Duquesne as though from a great distance.

"The older places don't, usually."

"In this climate, too." Temple shook his head disapprovingly. However, despite the bitter wind now blowing, he managed to look overheated, in his expensive crumpled suit, his stringy tie.

"You are staying on in Canberra, aren't you?" Temple looked anxious suddenly. "It would be more convenient for me if some problem or other arises."

"Yes, I'm stationed here now."

"Your wife is very beautiful. And you and she could pass for twins. Except that she is beautiful." Temple said the words reverently.

"Miss Grigorieva is not my wife, as it happens."

"I beg your pardon. She is not Australian, however."

"No. That is, she is a new Australian."

"Is she French?"

"She is of Russian parents."

"Has she by chance lived in France?"

"If you like to ask her, she will tell you that she was born in Russia, but was taken as a child to Paris by her mother. Her father was forced to remain behind. She lived in Paris until she was fourteen. She and her mother then moved to Rome. Ten years ago, on her mother's death, she came to Australia. Shall we return to business?"

Without reaction to the snub, Temple agreed to the inflated rental Duquesne was asking, which had already lost him two would-be tenants.

"Could I move in immediately?"

"Give me two days," said Duquesne. "I'm just back in Canberra and I have to move my stuff from the study. I'll meet you here Tuesday evening at five with the keys and the legal papers."

"I must get off. I told the cab to wait."

Irina came back to the kitchen then, and Temple bowed over her hand.

Together, Irina and Duquesne watched Temple down the path.

"He is shaped just like an egg," said Irina. "He's a sad egg, isn't he?"

Duquesne laughed, and his hand rose to entwine her neck. As he drew her close, her big shoulder-bag slipped down her arm and hit the bricks of the veranda with a crash. The bag came open, and its contents spilled. Irina bent hastily to pick up a very small camera.

Duquesne took it from her.

"Very classy. I'd no idea you were a photographer."

"I'm not really—just learning."

"You'll need to learn a lot to use this, I should think. Where did you get it?"

She said vaguely: "It was a present."

"Very new and no brand name," said Duquesne. With sudden intuition he added: "Is this what Vasily Sanin gave you this morning, just as I arrived at Timara?"

"Of course not," she laughed, not quite truly, and felt an unexpected blush begin to form.

"It's nothing to do with me, of course," Duquesne added, "if you want to accept presents from that pin-up boy."

"I could see you did not like him," she said lazily.

"What! Not like that combination of European courtliness and intelligent conversation! It's not his fault he's a pompous ass," said Duquesne, surprising himself as much as Irina with this offensiveness.

Precisely at that moment the telephone rang in the hall behind them. Duquesne disregarded it at first, then wrenched his eyes away from hers and walked over to it. Picking up the receiver, his wife's voice said: "Jack, what luck to get you. Forrest was a last resort."

"Hello there. How are you?" His voice became perceptibly gentler, and he hunched his shoulders, turning his back on Irina.

Meg said: "It's Jane's birthday in exactly two weeks. The third is a Saturday. You're coming, aren't you?"

"Lord, yes. Yes, of course."

She talked on for a little, and he listened in silence, then said: "I'll make it by midday. Don't worry. Everything all right? Take care of yourself."

Irina had thrown herself on to a chaise-longue, and gave him a look from her narrow eyes.

"It's nearly four o'clock, Jack. Can we go to Rosedale now? Now you've done with your egg?"

"I meant to tell you before, but I haven't had a chance. Rosedale is off, I'm afraid."

"Oh, no!" She sprang up. "I so wanted to get away . . . from everything."

"Something has come up for tomorrow afternoon."

"Sunday afternoon! Whatever is it?"

"Eh? Oh, just some work I have to do."

"I see." Her smile was ironic. "So you are standing me up?"

"This came up after our arrangement. I can't avoid it."

"Don't worry, Jack. . . ." She had already run down the steps to the car. He followed her, cursing.

"You might have told me, I think, before I took the trouble to come in to Canberra."

"We can have tonight. . . ."

"I think I'd better not intrude further on your weekend." Her voice was bright and determined. She opened the car door, then suddenly slipped off the red sweater and handed it to him.

"For God's sake, are you an adult or a child?" he exclaimed in exasperation.

She got into her MG and slammed the door viciously. Then she burst into tears, and his anger fled.

Drawing her out of the car, he said: "We *can* go to the coast. I wasn't lying or standing you up. But I must be back by tomorrow midday at latest. It's a very important appointment. I have to go and see the Prime Minister."

Later that evening, when they were locked in the swaying, vibrating world of the coast road, with the writhing gums, white and black and red, rushing at them in the glare of the Alfa's headlamps, barbed-wire fences endlessly unwinding, Irina said: "I did not mean to be so . . . inquisitive. I do not like inquisitive people."

"I know you didn't."

"The Prime Minister. . . . Oh, Jack, you *are* important," she said simply. "There's so much I don't know about you, even though we've already shared so much—like a whole life, split down the middle."

"There's not much to know. I've spent so much time these last years up-country, and in laboratories and offices and lecture rooms."

"With good results, I see, if you spend Sunday afternoon with the Prime Minister."

"A bit of work I've been doing has interested the powers that be, that's all. Please don't tell anyone."

He would not be drawn to say more, and they fell silent, while the bush closed in on them, graceless by night—and cruel.

# CHAPTER SEVEN

"DON'T MISUNDERSTAND ME," said the Minister for Science to the executive secretary of CSIRO, Sir John Doughty. "Testing will continue, but in conditions of the utmost secrecy. We leave the scientific details to you, of course, but our impression—the impression of the Prime Minister and his closest advisers—is that all the steps which have been taken by Dr. Duquesne should be repeated independently, one by one, and, following that, consecutive tests undertaken to establish vulnerability to disease and all other problems of practical application."

Turton paused and then said heavily: "Moreover, the Prime Minister wants you yourself to take charge of it."

"It is most unorthodox," said Doughty. "Dr. Duquesne is a distinguished man. His work is valuable. To take him off his own discovery is surely a slap in his face."

"You will not know, of course, but the Prime Minister himself has already spoken to Duquesne, who accepts the course of action which I am outlining now. It is entirely in the interests of national security—even for his own protection. And for the safeguarding of Australia's reputation."

The Minister's fleshy face began to mesmerise Sir John, as Turton embarked on a careful speech full of "immensely complex issues" and "implications beyond the purely scientific." Could Doughty trust his eyes, as Turton's moustache appeared to keep time with his speech?

Turton continued without emotion: "The results of these long-term and thoroughly responsible checks may well indicate an unstable aspect of the apparent positive qualities reported by Duquesne. It would be so easy for mistaken hopes to be raised, with incalculable political damage to ourselves and—er—those on whom we depend.

The exercise of policy responsibility in a matter like this demands the utmost caution. . . ."

Doughty listened in silence. Disbelief gave way to anger. Turton talked on for a while. . . .

Outside Parliament House once more, Doughty told the chauffeur of his Commonwealth car to wait and he walked down to the edge of the lake. Over in front of Parliament House a protest meeting with banners was getting under way; about a hundred Aborigines stood near a couple of temporary shacks which they called their headquarters. "DON'T TAKE OUR LAND FROM US," said one banner, in letters a foot high.

Doughty paced up and down beside the water's edge. He was in no doubt as to the practical implications of the policy directive which had just been given him by his Minister. It meant that ahead lay at least ten years or even more of restricted testing undertaken with the utmost secrecy. It meant that Duquesne would receive no public recognition of his work. Doughty wondered if Duquesne had recognised all the implications of what he had agreed to.

It was 180° different from Doughty's own recommendation. It offended the professional standards of his discipline. He was unsure whether this promising discovery would in fact ever see the light of day, whether it would ever be given the chance of fulfilling its potential contribution as a great additional source of food. Was he, therefore, justified in accepting the directive of his Minister?

Never in his long and honourable career had he been faced with such a decision. It was true that in the past he had been required once or twice to modify his own ideas for the application of scientific advances, but they had been matters parochial by comparison.

It was also true that it was the Government which made policy and it was the moral obligation of senior servants of the country such as he to carry out those policies, even when personally they held different views. It was equally recognised that in any society worthy of respect no man could be forced to take actions which were utterly repugnant to him. Was this such a case? Sir John shook his head wearily. Life was much simpler in his years as a scientist. He preferred the laboratory to the administrative office and high advisory position.

He could decline to accept the directive, in which case the only honourable course would be to resign. But he well knew that he was not the sort of man who—unlike some others—would subsequently publish memoirs based on his inside knowledge. His standards were the old ones; they required that he keep silent. In this case, his successor would be faced with the same directive, and it was unlikely that a much younger successor would jeopardise his new appointment. Nor would he have the background experience to justify an effective opposition to the government view.

Finally, Sir John was only a year off retirement, and if he resigned now his pension would be gravely reduced. Did he want to go out and begin a career once again at his age? Did he have the right to impose this sacrifice on the family he had started as a middle-aged man?

At the end of a long hour Sir John had made his choice and walked with decision back to his car. From its telephone he told his secretary to call Duquesne into his office.

By the time Sir John reached his office, Duquesne was already waiting. The two men entered the inner room. Doughty looked searchingly at the scientist. He liked Duquesne's leanness and intelligence of face, the refinements of feature which a long line of European intellectuals had bestowed. The eyes were bright blue and brilliant behind spectacles. Against his will Sir John's thoughts returned to the years when he, too, was a scientist in his thirties, intent on the excitement and challenges of his work.

Emotion made his voice brusque and harsh.

"Dr. Duquesne. I understand the Prime Minister has spoken to you and told you it is necessary to limit the testing of your new wheat strain to Australia and to observe the utmost secrecy. There will be no release of news concerning it."

Duquesne said, through tight lips: "That's so, sir."

Sir John relaxed his almost unconscious stiffness.

"Your work has been magnificent, Dr. Duquesne. I'm full of admiration." Momentarily unselfish enthusiasm came through. "I can imagine your disappointment now."

Duquesne's lips sketched an ironic smile.

"I admit I was already practically on my way to our new centre for technical aid to the developing countries, sir," he replied. "Of course

I'm disappointed we have to go ahead in this hole-and-corner manner, especially as the scientific world is hell-bent on developing tropical food grains by all manner of means—nitrogen fixation and so on. And my wheat promises a yield equal to those only being dreamed of by these scientists. The Australian government no doubt have very valid reasons for what they are doing. At least I hope they have."

With an effort Duquesne curbed his tongue and stared across at Sir John, whom he admired.

Since Sunday afternoon in the garden of the Lodge, with Blantyre pouring him tea, speaking man to man, with no one else present, the elation which Duquesne had felt from that brief hour behind the scenes had faded. The Prime Minister had talked of the fight against hunger, of certain developing countries which both he and Duquesne knew at firsthand. He had talked of Australia's status in the world and of her reputation for scientific and technological excellence. He had talked of the anti-communist struggle which still continued and he had, surprisingly, touched very fluently on the undesirability of Australia appearing to support the Lysenko theory that the heredity of organisms can be changed by directed training, that Marxism will produce better social beings.

The Prime Minister had then spoken of the disastrous effects for poor countries of large-scale adoption of a new wheat which later proved a failure. To protect those countries, to protect Australia's reputation, he wanted all-out testing—but this to be done in Australia. It had to be done thoroughly and in conditions of absolute secrecy. Testing would be intensified, the scale enlarged, but it would be confined to Australia. Then, when finally they were sure of the value of the new wheat, news of it would be released.

Without the powerful personality of the man himself to bolster his arguments, those arguments had since tottered. Duquesne knew now he had been propelled relentlessly towards agreement with a decision which he felt at bottom to be wrong. And a promise had been extracted from him, as from a pygmy in the hands of a giant.

"I can't", he said to Sir John Doughty, "really comprehend the potential implications at the international level. At least, I was immensely reassured when the Prime Minister said you would be taking over responsibility directly. It shows that the Government is giving due importance to the wheat."

Sir John stared at him uneasily and muttered: "Yes, well . . ."

"Is absolute secrecy even feasible, sir?" Duquesne ventured. "Can extensive testing be kept secret? And are funds available? I mean, on an expensive security basis?"

"Oh, they'll be forthcoming. Drawn from innocent-sounding appropriations in the budgets of several departments," muttered Sir John vaguely. "Governments always have their slush funds."

Then he fell silent, his face set.

Duquesne said, rather tentatively: "It's very much in your old field, sir. I'd like to help."

Sir John's lips came firmly together.

"Thank you. When I need you, I'll let you know."

"As for my future work, sir . . ."

"Your work on rice will continue to take care of the next few months, I understand. If you have any suggestions, feel perfectly free to make them. Don't forget our world of science is infinitely large, with infinite possibilities. You are one of the few who has shown that he can recognise and exploit an opportunity for scientific advance." He considered for a moment. "Why not take some time off? You must surely need a rest now."

Duquesne smiled.

"I usually go underwater-exploring for relaxation. Life is simple down there—and clean. But I could use some leave for another purpose, too. I have been asked to take part in a UN meeting on grains to be held in Rome next month. I would be one of the group of independent experts advising the meeting. Would it be in order if I went and added a few more weeks as leave?"

Sir John nodded unthinkingly.

"Yes, indeed. Nothing simpler. Of course you have to respect bureaucratic formalities, so make your application and give it in to Beattie."

After a little more small talk, Duquesne left.

Doughty picked up his telephone and told his secretary that he was not to be disturbed for any reason whatsoever for the next hour. Then he went to his sideboard and for the first time in a career of almost forty years he poured himself a large glass of whisky and sat down in his office to drink it alone.

# CHAPTER EIGHT

When Duquesne reached his house at Forrest on Tuesday night, Dick Temple was already there. He had paid off his taxi and was standing in the porch, a lonely fat man surrounded by three battered suitcases which still hinted at their expensive origin.

"I'm late," said Duquesne.

"Not too much so." Temple's face brightened. "That one," he gestured towards the street, "didn't find it, either. Had to instruct him." He showed Duquesne a map of Canberra. "I guess Walter Burley Griffin is usually the winner." His shoulders shook slightly at what he evidently considered a verbal jump ahead.

Going into the house with him, Duquesne wondered again if Temple's wife wanted all that space for entertaining. "I'm afraid I haven't moved my books out yet," he said apologetically. "A friend is coming along with his station-wagon to help move them."

Their business was quickly done, the lease signed, the contents of the house checked against the inventory. A prosperous man (for such the number of Temple's credit cards and bankers' references suggested him to be), he seemed the ideal tenant. Duquesne also noted the efficiency underlying the seemingly casual manners. A minor error in dating was observed, corrected and initialled all in a moment.

"We could have a drink, to celebrate," said Temple, almost anxiously. He brought out from a suitcase a bottle of Scotch. "I buy Cutty Sark only because of the advertisements," he joked.

They sat one each side of the kitchen table. Temple pulled out an evening paper and showed Duquesne a headline.

"Your government is threatening a hard line on the trade union people," he said.

"Yes, the unions are mostly anti-uranium. It might come to a direct challenge to the Government's authority if they bring the troops in."

"I guess we both have the same division of power between government, unions and big business interests. Personally I back the business interests."

Duquesne, thinking of the tough alert face which had faced him in the grounds of the Prime Minister's Lodge on Sunday, nodded.

"As a scientist I'm probably not much of a judge. Most of us scientific blokes keep to our own lines," he said.

"Ah, yes. I'm really the same. M'father had some land that proved more valuable for urban development than for agriculture, so I guess I'm just a little old farmer without a farm."

Duquesne wondered if Temple was serious.

"But you've come to Canberra—at least for a while. That's an odd choice."

Temple delicately skirted the implied question.

"Quite a number of us Americans are attracted to your country," he said. "It's big, like ours, but without so many people. And you might not believe it, but not so much government, either. Thought I might do a little of this and a little of that, help to bring our two fine countries closer together and perhaps earn a few dollars in the process." Again his shoulders shook in what was apparently an indication of mirth. "I do have some connections with agricultural and with marine interests, and they would like to be better informed. As it happens, they're my hobbies, too. Oh, I really want to see your coastline and do a bit of underwater exploring."

His eyes sought the kitchen wall behind Duquesne's head, where Duquesne knew still hung his favourite photograph of himself holding a marlin which he had just speared. Meg had hung it there years ago.

"It's not too typical of my activities now," said Duquesne. "I'm more of an undersea naturalist than fisherman nowadays."

"I saw your other photographs in the hall. Where do you fish?"

"Nearest place to Canberra is down the coast, Batemans Bay way. I have a small place not far from there."

"Is that so? I guess I'll get myself a car and drive myself round a little. I don't care for this side of the road, but you folk seem to manage it." His shoulders shook only slightly. "I've fished in Bermuda."

"Scuba or spear-fishing?"

"The bottle."

"Bermuda has a fine reputation."

"Almost ideal conditions. Reefs—coral reefs, with fish of every sort you can think of. The reefs break the heavy seas. You fish the first reef-belt, and then you are not troubled by sharks and barracuda, which I have heard is the case in Australian waters."

"They don't bother you if you don't bother them."

Temple emitted a great laugh.

"Oh! That's good! That would relieve any stranger's mind." His eyes went to the door behind Duquesne and he rose, saying: "You've come at the opportune moment, sir."

Duquesne grinned at the big balding man who had entered by the back door, saying to Dick: "Meet Jerry Hill. He is recently back from the Barrier Reef. He can tell you about sharks. Groper, too."

Duquesne rented his Hackett apartment from Jerry, though this was only incidental to a friendship dating from schooldays. Between them was a solid bond of shared experience, including treks by jeep into the interior and a whole world of underwater spear-fishing.

Jerry accepted a drink and said: "Nasty chap, the groper. A shark always circles before attacking. The groper lurks among the coral caves and from there suddenly rushes you. Every once in a while a big groper takes an Abo or half of him in one bite. . . ."

Jerry seemed to take possession of the kitchen, with his shirt—a garish red which hurt the eyes—dragged tightly over his barrel chest, his strong face with its obstinate set to chin and lips, his racy but elaborate diction.

Duquesne glanced at his watch an hour and several drinks later and said: "I'd like to hear what Blantyre has to say. He's talking about uranium in two minutes' time." He switched on a television set on the kitchen dresser. Since his visit to the Prime Minister's Lodge he felt intense curiosity about Blantyre, and now he waited impatiently.

The screen flickered into life, and suddenly Prime Minister Blantyre was talking. It was a short speech and an earnest one. He spoke first of the Aborigines in the uranium area of the Northern Territory. "Their welfare, their interests, are of vital concern to my government," he told his listeners. "You may be certain that both protection of their sacred sites and title to their traditional land are assured."

About uranium, the Prime Minister was equally serious and compelling.

"Australia has at least twenty per cent of the world's high-grade uranium reserves. Uranium is and will remain the most accessible source of additional power for at least the remainder of the century.

"I reject the sort of criticism I have had from opponents who consider exploitation of uranium to be against the interests of poor nations. They work to death the basically false contrast 'maintaining the life styles of the affluent when we should be more concerned to help feed the world's hungry.'

"First, poor countries, too, need increasing supplies of energy. In a world seriously short of energy, they would be the first to suffer because energy prices would go up even more steeply. How much oil does OPEC sell cheaply to them? None. Energy from nuclear power in the rich countries will increase total world supplies and keep down prices of energy.

"Second, you must understand that bringing down the standard of living of the rich countries—which is what lack of energy would mean—inevitably damages the poor countries. And you all know which rich country has for decades given—and still gives—enormously of aid in all forms to those less fortunate—the country to whom Australia herself looks first for co-operation and support. I mean the United States of America, our nuclear ally.

"And, again, I am in full agreement with the President of the United States that safeguarding against the proliferation of nuclear weapons is one of the most important international issues of today. Only as a supplier of uranium to the United States or to countries adhering to her nuclear standards can Australia be an effective force in achieving improved international safeguards and controls.

"The export of Australian uranium will help make a safer world."

The eyes of the Prime Minister bored into them for some moments after he had finished speaking, owing to some slight technical hitch in the camera room.

"How's that for support? You must feel more at home here already." Jerry glanced at Dick. "Back in Johnson's time it used to be 'All the way with LBJ'. Now . . ."

"Our government certainly wants the United States to buy our uranium," said Duquesne. "If the price is a good one, we should be able to give a quid pro quo."

Temple started and stared at Duquesne.

"The Prime Minister has got to mine," Duquesne went on. "He's committed to it. His whole political future rests on the big business interests." He added slyly: "Of course, Australia could well afford not to mine. She's rich enough." He knew that Jerry, a wealthy man, owned some half a million dollars of mining shares.

"And would there be any point in Australia alone abstaining from uranium mining?" asked Temple.

"The example she would set to the rest of the world. With all these uranium reserves, she would attract enormous attention."

"Example my arse. We can't any longer depend simply on oil." Jerry's vehemence was born only partly of drink. "I'd even question the morality of leaving it in the ground."

"*Is* there an energy supply crisis? You know," said Duquesne owlishly, "I'm inclined to think not. But there may be an energy use crisis."

He stopped and said: "Who's this?"

Unnoticed, an intense-looking man had been speaking on the television for some moments in a very English voice.

"These Aboriginal people have lived in the area for at least twenty-five thousand years. There can be no compromise with the problem. The white invasion of miners and their retinue will be fatal. Only in isolation from the whites can the Aborigines of Australia live out their strange and indeed unique lives, act according to their own standards, preserve their ancient traditions. Put them with whites and they are beset by terrible problems—not least of which is drink. Assimilation is not possible. Mine uranium and the doom of this ancient race is sealed. . . ."

Duquesne said grimly: "He's right."

He had had contact with Aborigines up north, and his sympathy and compassion were deep.

"Are they so numerous?" asked Temple.

"Only about eight hundred, up in that particular part of the Territory," Duquesne replied.

Temple drawled: "You don't really expect a handful of blacks to hold things up, do you? Or think they ought to? I thought their doom, by all accounts, was sealed long ago by your countrymen." Something out of character and very hard showed momentarily behind Temple's eyes—before his usual blandness came back.

"No, I don't expect it," returned Duquesne. "Their opposition to mining is likely to be ineffective, but they see the Ranger mining project as an act of aggression and, even if they agree finally on paper, it will only be from despair and the knowledge that nothing will deter the Government. It's quite shameful."

He rose and said abruptly: "I'd better get on to the books."

In the study, where his library—contained in six steel sets of shelves—awaited his attention, Temple ambled after him, reluctant to let him go.

"I guess I can give you a hand. This will take some moving. You have a real library." Temple peered at titles.

Duquesne, who had sat down at his desk, did not answer. He had switched on a desk lamp and sat staring at the accumulation of papers on the desktop. The top one, he was annoyed to note, was a report on Le Duc 1980 which he had forgotten to lock away. Automatically, his hand went to his pocket and closed over the key to the locked cabinet containing his wheat seeds. The cabinet was still safely locked.

" 'An Alkaline Water Retention Capacity Test for the Evaluation of Baking Potentialities of Soft Winter Wheat Flours.' How really marvellous a title." Temple burbled now, walking round and reading book titles. Duquesne sat quite still at his desk. Temple looked round enquiringly.

Still without a word, Duquesne pulled open drawers and checked through papers for some minutes.

"Anything wrong?" drawled Temple.

"Someone's been at my desk."

"You missing something?"

"No. The top papers aren't in the order that I left them in. And the lamp has been changed to throw its light differently."

"You might be mistaken."

"No." Duquesne uttered the word so savagely that Temple froze.

"Perhaps the cleaning woman . . ."

"There isn't a cleaning woman. And the house has been locked up. I've only been using this study now and then."

"Whoever it was had to get in to do it."

Duquesne said nothing. He sensed disbelief, amusement even, on Temple's part, and went white with anger. Abruptly he rose and began a rapid inspection of every window and door in the house. Temple and Jerry followed him. All the locks and catches were in order. Back in the study, Duquesne rechecked drawers and desktop.

"Well?" asked Jerry, who had remained silent until then.

"No one would have noticed it but me. But there's no mistake. Someone has been at my papers."

"So your ghost had a key?" asked Temple.

Duquesne said, without looking at him: "The two sets I'm handing over to you today are the only keys."

The three men did the packing and dismantled the shelving. With Temple's help they made short work of it. A fat man Temple might be, but he handled the heavy steel pieces as though they were part of a Meccano set.

As Duquesne and Jerry took their leave, Temple said: "I hope your ghost doesn't have it in for me." The shoulders shook very faintly.

Glancing back, they carried with them the picture of Temple standing in the middle of the lawn, a curious figure, his hands, after the manner of fat men, loosely at his sides.

Over in the Hackett apartment, Duquesne and Jerry unloaded the books and shelving.

"I'll do something about the front-door lock here. It's very shaky." Jerry roamed round checking the condition of the flat. He owned a number of houses and flats, the acquiring of which, together with his gambling on the share market, served as outlet for a business acumen not called upon by his job in a government department. Argumentative and difficult, he was slowly creating his own isolation. He was nobody's friend, Duquesne sometimes suspected, except Duquesne's.

Duquesne shrugged.

"I haven't much to steal here. People don't steal books."

Jerry scowled.

"But they seem interested in your papers."

As they re-erected the shelving, Jerry asked: "Ever come across a chap called Brent?"

"No."

"He seemed to know you." Jerry's eyes wandered. "Ken Brent, of Defence. I've known him for years. Or let's say he's been known to me for years. If you get the fine distinction." Pushing his lips forward in a characteristic grimace, Jerry added: "A damn inquisitive bastard."

When, an hour later, and a little drunk by now, Jerry took his leave, he slapped Duquesne over the shoulder and said emphatically and unexpectedly: "You never know what bastard has it in for you. By God, Jack, I'll tell you one thing. They can pester me as much as they like, but they'll get no information out of me. You can rest easy on that score."

"Do you mean Brent? *What* has he been trying to get out of you?"

"Information about your work."

Duquesne started.

"But he could find out so easily from other sources. From me, for instance!"

"Yeah. Well, he wanted to know all sorts of other things, too. Personal details. . . . Whether you drink."

"What did you say?"

"I told him to bugger off." Jerry was suddenly diffident. His eyes were worried as he glanced at Duquesne. "What's it all about?"

"If I knew, I'd tell you," said Duquesne heavily.

"I'll fix your locks up anyway. Next weekend I'm tied up. Saturday morning after that."

And Jerry left the apartment. Revving up his Volkswagen stationwagon and shooting down the drive with a terrific roar, he narrowly missed an oncoming bus as he turned into Majura Avenue. Duquesne shuddered. Jerry, so careful, even parsimonious, in small things, was prodigal with cars. He had smashed up at least six.

Duquesne went inside. For the disarrangement of his papers in Forrest he hoped to find an innocent explanation. But Brent remained. And he thought again of his wife saying to him on the phone a few nights before: "He was a big man, foreign, and he said he was writing an article on wheat. He wanted to know all about your work. How could he have known where I lived?"

# CHAPTER NINE

THE FOLLOWING MONDAY, Duquesne was called from the laboratory to answer a personal call on the phone. "My name is Street. I'm just down from the Top End. You remember Charlie? Charlie Connors? I have something I should pass on to you from him. Could we meet?"

A full rich voice with breezy compelling tones, it spelled, unmistakably, Melbourne private school. Caught by surprise, Duquesne agreed to meet the voice that evening at the Hotel Civic.

Later on he looked with some distaste on the slightly built man who rose to meet him in the hotel lounge. The same big voice did not go with Mr. Street's lack of size and general jumpiness.

"I had to visit Canberra, so I thought I'd look you up." Street beckoned to the waiter, saying: "No, this is on me. What'll you have?"

"You're in the uranium business, Mr. Street?" Duquesne thought it unlikely.

The other pursed his lips and shook his head.

"I represent the Business and General Assurance Company in insurance of heavy vehicles, including earth-moving machinery. I was up at the Ranger uranium site for a few days and had to see Charlie in the course of this business."

He did not explain further. The waiter was not keeping up with his orders, and Street's eyes slid after the man as he skidded with his tray among the tables, banging down glasses and fumbling one-handed with change. Street rapped impatiently on the table.

"You have something for me from Charlie?" enquired Duquesne.

"A message. You know he's left the Ranger?"

"What! Left the . . . ? You mean he's gone back to his farm on the Daly?"

"So you hadn't heard? No, I didn't mean that. Ah, that's better."

Street sketched a salute with his glass and let half the beer just served slip down his throat.

"When did he leave?" Duquesne asked.

"More than three weeks ago. A Saturday. The fifth of April it would have been. The story was put about that he was sick. In fact he was right as rain. I think myself he was turned off. You know, of course, that he was paid through CSIRO?"

"Why do you think he was turned off?" Duquesne asked sharply.

"Because he was so different when I caught up with him again in Darwin. That's when he gave me the message for you. I mentioned I had to go to Canberra, and he said would I find you and tell you how sorry he was to have left the job, and how badly he felt about it. He was a nice old chap. I felt I could oblige him."

"Surely he told you *why* he left!"

"He simply said he was buying a property near his brother, down in New South Wales. But he'd never said a word of it up till the time he left." Street's eyes flicked continuously away and back to Duquesne's face. "For some odd reason, he had been suddenly paid off with almost a golden handshake. Wish I could get the same."

"A golden handshake!" Duquesne looked at the other in surprise.

"Queer show," said Street reflectively. "He was overflowing with money. Of course, another queer thing was the fire. I wonder sometimes if there was a connection between that and Charlie's leaving."

"Fire? What fire?" Duquesne asked, puzzled.

"Of course, it's only what I've been told." Street watched covertly for a reaction from Duquesne. "But apparently it was just on a week ago, on a Tuesday night—out at that godforsaken experimental plot which Charlie looked after."

"Experimental plot? What happened?" Duquesne's personality seemed to swell and advance menacingly. Street hurriedly set down his glass.

"Several people told me. It seems that towards midnight there was a sudden blaze in this area. Fire prevention officers went there, but were turned away. Kaput. Finished. No use."

"What the hell do you mean?" Duquesne demanded.

"Don't blame me, for Heaven's sake," Street begged. This bloody scientist did look dangerous. All brains, no balance. He said cautiously and slowly, watching Duquesne intently: "Apparently there was some sort of experimental plot which burned up unexpectedly. Or was burned up. That's all. The rest is hearsay. The area itself was kept strictly off limits." His voice held a trace of resentment.

"This was Tuesday? The twenty-second?"

Street nodded.

"You said Charlie left three weeks ago—that is, over two weeks before this fire, which was six days ago. What possible connection can there be?"

"Perhaps there isn't. It's only that each incident is in itself odd, don't you think? And Charlie was working on this—er—experimental crop."

Duquesne, staring hard at Street, caught a look almost of amusement at the back of Street's eyes, a look of such wise, almost paternal intelligence that he was taken aback. For a moment Street's face seemed to pull together, the too mobile features to cement, so that the head was suddenly a well-shaped one, the face even good-looking.

"Charlie thinks the world of you, you know," said Street.

And then, in a second, the furtive expression returned, as, with a hand which might well have been clean but looked grubby, he put the rest of his drink to his wet lips, rose and said to Duquesne pleasantly: "Anyway, I'm off to find him. He's somewhere near Griffith. I'll leave you my Sydney telephone number. We might have cause to get in touch again on Charlie's account."

Street gave Duquesne a card, a plain white card, on which he had scribbled "John F. Street" and a number. It was not a business card.

Later that evening, Duquesne sat opposite Dick Temple in the Singapore, a big plain L-shaped restaurant in a south-side suburb, with white tablecloths and black chairs, staffed by dark little men with brilliant-white smiles. It was Dick's find. He had even provided transport—a 1974 VW saloon which he had just bought—and had joked all the way over from Hackett at his successful handling of this compact car. He had practised the gears all day.

Duquesne was glad of Dick tonight. A meal with him as host had to be lengthy. He watched him fiddle with the cutlery, pour wine liberally, and listened to his now familiar approach to a subject—his puckish disarray of facts, the seemingly artless manipulation of ideas and then the swift logical conclusion. The wine was a 1975 Pokolbin, two bottles. He was doing Duquesne proud in every respect, and seemed almost to be courting him at times, until in an instant the impression vanished, now at a turn of Dick's head, to reveal the straight and arrogant nose, the drooping eyelids, or now at a view expressed with more than usually careless enunciation.

And while they talked Duquesne was conducting another conversation which never quite got under way—sometimes with Beattie, sometimes with Sir John Doughty. Duquesne spoke of the fire. "I've just heard of it. It is incredible to me that I was not informed. After nearly a week. . . ."

They said various things in reply, reasonable or even plausible, but none fully convincing.

After the second bottle of Pokolbin, Dick began to talk of spearfishing, of the equipment he had just bought in Sydney, and a film of unreality closed over the evening, dulling care. They finished their sukiyaki and ate exotic fruits and sweetmeats, drank coffee, and drove a little waveringly to Forrest to inspect the new equipment. There they sampled Dick's French brandy before Dick ran Duquesne to Hackett, where in turn they sampled Duquesne's Australian brandy. Standing out in the courtyard, they noisily agreed on an expedition to the sea at Rosedale on Saturday week. By this time, Duquesne knew that he would sleep out the seven hours before he faced Beattie, or else Sir John, and the consequent showdown from which no good could possibly come.

"Did you know the wheat had been destroyed?"

Duquesne was finally facing Beattie across the latter's desk. Beattie's friendly gaze froze on his face.

"Only very recently. I've been desperately busy all week, Jack." Beattie fished round on his desk for a file, pursed his lips, then, slapping a hand on the table in irritation, came on the file in a drawer. "A letter came in the other day." He rustled papers and tossed it over. "You take this as a serious setback, do you?" He sounded faintly surprised. "I don't, you see. And I don't know whether you know, but at least a couple of dozen plants are safe. Robertson sent them down to the Katherine experimental station."

"I'm afraid," said Duquesne, keeping a tight rein on himself, "that I *do* see the burning of a whole trial plot as a setback. Since the man looking after the plot was turned off *weeks* before, perhaps it's hardly surprising the plot came to grief!"

"Yes." Beattie was vague. "I haven't got the background to that yet. But it's not very important now."

"Not important . . ." Duquesne's voice trembled.

"I understand how you feel, Jack," Beattie broke in hastily, "but it's not your responsibility any longer. And you must surely be relieved that those plants are safe. Dobbs says they are in very good condition."

"And yet no one bothered to inform me."

"I'm sorry about that. Just the pressure of work. Nothing else."

"Don't talk crap," said Duquesne, without thinking.

Beattie pretended not to hear and clapped him on the back.

"Care to come along and have a drink with Marj and me tonight?"

"I'm tied up, thanks," Duquesne said ungraciously. He handed a paper to Beattie and said: "There's a UN meeting on grains at the FAO on the second of June. I'd like to attend, as I did the last one. I've written out a formal application for this and additional leave. Sir John said I should give it to you. In the circumstances CSIRO can easily get along without me for a few weeks."

Beattie took the memorandum without comment, and Duquesne added: "I've got to hurry."

He knew, as he said goodnight and walked out of the office, that Beattie was standing looking after him.

# CHAPTER TEN

"I GRIEVE for our lost weekend," Irina said on Friday night, looking at Duquesne over an omelette she had cooked in the Hackett flat. "We must have a specially good wine to console me."

Duquesne was catching a late plane to Sydney that night to see Jane, whose birthday it was the next day. He knew that Irina was jealous and was relieved that she seemed to be taking it well.

"What will you do?" he asked.

"I will stay at the stables all through. So I shan't see you till next Friday."

Her blonde hair shone under the unshaded lamp as she held up a glass of wine he poured for her, contrasting with the rich red of the Tyrell's Hunter Valley.

"You choose to go away, so the god grape will comfort me." She abruptly changed the subject, saving Duquesne from making what could only be a limp reply. "How is your fat man?" she asked.

"He is comfortably installed, together with his dishwasher, but is at least as demanding of my time as the office."

Duquesne's evenings, surprisingly, had been largely given up to Dick Temple in the previous ten days. Duquesne would go to help with the oil heater or some other practical problem, but Temple kept him to talk. The bottle of Scotch would be brought out, and there would follow the long conversations, meandering through the highways and byways of Temple's experience rather than Duquesne's. A talker of wide range, he threw out statements either provocative or eccentric, giving rise to the curious verbal give and take which was more contest than discussion. His fat man's laughter was never far away, as he surrounded Duquesne with his web of suggestion and question, drawing him out on his work, professional responsibility, his view of major current issues.

"He is at the Embassy?"

"No. He is a rich man and is thinking of settling here."

"Why would he want to settle in Canberra?"

"Well, this is the capital city. Then he likes underwater fishing and he can get to the coast easily." Duquesne paused, then added a little sadly: "You don't like this country very much, do you?"

"Oh, you fool. I love it! It's not Europe, that's all." Her voice was full of suppressed longing. "I just want to be there again for a while . . . where there is a struggle going on!"

"Yes, I think I understand you." Duquesne could not think who else had said much the same to him recently.

"His wife is not here yet?" Irina was asking.

"In spirit only. Oh, and in a silver-framed picture which has the place of honour on the baby grand piano. Permanent wave and pearls and a royal smile. A WASP, like him."

"What?"

"White, Anglo-Saxon, Protestant. The establishment class, particularly of the Eastern States. He carries the photograph with him, you see, as other men wear a wedding ring. As a protection."

She glanced instinctively at his hands, and he found himself saying: "Would you come to Rome with me?"

"Oh, Jack!" Her voice was full of longing. "*Would* I!"

"I'm invited to a UN meeting on the second of June. We'll make plans when I get back from Sydney. You arrange to be away from the stables for at least a month."

She insisted, then, on opening another bottle of wine, which they finished afterwards in bed. A short while later, as she was driving him to the airport, he half-regretted the second bottle. But only half.

She was volubly happy, and he felt he had allayed her jealous fears. He wondered why she wept a little as she said goodbye.

Duquesne returned from Sydney midday Sunday—earlier than he had expected—depressed and carrying with him a picture of Jane waiting for him on the steps of Bexley House School for Girls at Cremorne, her face anxious and taut, standing stiffly by herself amongst a crowd of milling girls. His wife had said, in her considered fashion: "I think

Jane is not doing too badly at school. She has to come out into the world one day and make the break."

Duquesne privately thought that Jane's mother alternated disastrously between overprotection and leaving her daughter too much alone. The form teacher looked a fool, and he doubted if the pretentious school could compete with an ordinary government school in Canberra. But what could he do? He surprised himself wondering if he and Irina might later have a daughter. At least Jane had obviously been overjoyed with the smart Minolta camera he had given her for her birthday. He must ask Irina about that unusual camera she carried.

Back in Hackett, he phoned Irina at once, but was told she had gone out of Canberra. They did not know where. She was not due back at the stables until Monday. He suddenly panicked, combing the apartment for a trace of her. But she had left nothing of herself.

He thought of Vasily Sanin, handing her down from her horse, his hand remaining too long. Had Irina walked out on him just when he was conscious of a desperate need?

The week's work caught him up, and thankfully he submitted. Thursday morning he had a call from Street. Street was in Sydney but would arrive in Canberra that afternoon. Duquesne arranged to see him at the Lakeside Hotel at seven o'clock. Later in the morning he read again a letter he had received days before from the Professor of History in the University of Melbourne, who was writing a massive book on Pacific affairs.

"I am trying", he wrote, "to get a clear picture of the likely food situation in certain Pacific countries over the next ten to twenty years. I need information about possible changes which might be brought about by scientific developments such as increased use of fertilisers, for instance, or new techniques of plant breeding. Sir John Doughty advised me to consult you.

"I shall be in Canberra Thursday morning together with a collaborator, and expect to stay over until Saturday night. I wonder if we might meet. I shall take the liberty of phoning you."

Normally the letter would have signalled only an unwelcome encroachment on his time. Now it was even valuable, in the world of shifting realities he inhabited, as concrete evidence of his identity as a man of science, honoured in his field.

Then, out of the blue, the switchboard girl buzzed through and said: "Miss Grigorieva is on the line wanting to talk to you if convenient."

"Miss who? Oh, put her on." And his heart leaped.

When Irina came on the line he said: "So—you've turned up at last." His voice came out reluctant and churlish.

"I had to do something, go away in a hurry."

"Of course, you're entirely free to do as you like."

She uttered an impatient exclamation.

"When did you get back?"

"I got back when I said." He was glad to rap the words out sternly and listen to how they sounded.

"Jack, I had to go off suddenly. To Sydney." Her voice was suddenly urgent. "Jack! Let us meet."

"All right. Tomorrow?"

"Tonight. I'll come in special. Specially."

The blood pounded in his head. With false reluctance he said: "I'll meet you at Civic, in Garema Place, at five."

He was there some minutes early, just in time to see her climb out of a car pulled up at the kerb. She bent down to speak to the driver, and he saw it was Vasily Sanin. The car pulled away.

She turned quickly and saw him at once. Her face shone, then died slowly at his expression. In her old raincoat, tightly belted, she was smarter than any of the primped-up government typists now streaming from their offices. He went and stood, unyielding and sullen, in front of her and said: "Well?"

The smile came again, tremulously, as she replied: "It was just something came up. Something I just had to do."

"With Sanin!"

"No, no."

"He dropped you here just now."

Her eyes widened.

"He gave me a ride in. My car is in the garage here for servicing. I pick it up in an hour."

A sudden bitter gust raked the street, and he said: "We'd better go and get something to eat."

Inside a café, they sat at a table set with red plastic mats. Noise bounced off dirty white walls.

Irina, clutching the menu, abstractedly ordered spaghetti bolognese.

"Don't let's be ridiculous, Jack! Let's forget it all." She rattled cutlery into place on the table, trying to sparkle, recklessly expending her charm.

She laughed at the dish the waitress brought and said: "It looks awful."

"You'll get better in Rome." Duquesne had the girl bring them some wine, and Irina talked on gallantly.

"It's not always so good, the Roman cooking. The oil is sometimes not true. You need to know where to go."

"We don't have to stay all the time in Rome." His anger was suddenly gone; his mood somersaulted inexplicably. "We can go some place. Florence. You like Florence."

"Oh, yes, it's always so beautiful, all of a piece, better than Rome. Rome," she said, and then, indistinctly, Duquesne caught the words, "our dream."

"Better than a dream, very soon now. The reality. Three weeks. Let us stop off in Hong Kong. I haven't been there since the days I used to make love with Chinese girls almost as beautiful as you."

"You tease me, yes? I know you do! Oh, Jack, let us do that."

Looking at her closely, he saw her eyes were wet with tears.

"Irina!" he said sharply.

"Oh, it will all be marvellous," she assured him, speaking a little jerkily. The tears rained down her face.

He paid the bill and hustled her out of the café to his car.

"Now, what's it all about?" he asked sternly. "It's as though you don't believe me when I say I'm going, that I want you to come. I thought you wanted to."

She clung to him like one possessed.

"I want to—I want to more than anything in the world." Her arms around him hurt.

"What do you feel for me?" she whispered, against his cheek.

"I don't want to tell you, not quite yet."

"Rome is a joyride, isn't it?"

"Don't spoil everything. You're like . . ."

"Like all other women, aren't I?"

"It's just precisely because you're *not,* but . . ."

"But you must be so cautious, so safe, so sure."

"It's not that really. I lead a complicated life at present."

"Yes! Of which I know nothing. Nothing at all. You've put me in one little corner and you take me out sometimes and play with me, that's all."

"Christ!" he muttered, thinking back over the last few days.

"And because I don't tell you where I am for two days," she said passionately, "you don't like it at all. And you go off to see your daughter and your wife, and that's all right, of course. Like all Australians—all Australian men. You're a real Australian, aren't you, Jack?"

"Shut up." He shook her a little and laughed. "You're all wrought up."

She burst once more into tears.

"Listen, Irina." He spoke carefully now. "You've got it all wrong. I think I'm at a sort of turning-point, but I can't hurry it. I'll tell you something. I didn't at all want to come back to Australia. I might very well leave Australia soon, because what was holding me here has lost its force."

"You mean your wife?"

"Oh, no. I told you. We're separated. I'm still legally married to her, but only for the sake of our daughter. I mean my work."

"Where would you go?"

Duquesne laughed shortly. "Wherever I can sell my services and put them to full use," he said harshly.

His grip tightened on her, and he cupped her face with his hands, forcing her to meet his eyes.

"Don't spoil it all. Don't try to hurry everything."

"Can I not share in your problems? I know nothing of your life."

"Believe me, for the time being, it's better that way."

After a pause, she said, sounding exhausted: "I have to pick up my car."

She stayed beside him, irresolute, after he drew up beside the Mort Street garage, her face gleaming palely, framed by the blonde waves of hair.

"We'll go to Rome, Irina. Perhaps in Rome everything will seem very much clearer."

He left her, feeling that he had been forced to think and speak in a way foreign to him up to now.

Irina walked into the garage, inspected her MG, settled the bill in the office, and drove up Mort Street until she saw a black Fiat parked with its parking lamps on. She flashed her own lights twice and pulled up in front of it. Then she sat and waited while a man got out of the other car and approached—a short thick figure in dark raincoat and hat.

He opened the door of the MG and got in beside Irina.

"Well?" The intermittent lights of passing cars lit up a heavy face with penetrating cold eyes.

"There was nothing of note in his apartment. The seed he must have somewhere else." She spoke in Russian.

"What has he been saying?"

"He talks of leaving Australia and going wherever his work can be fully used."

"He will go to the UN conference?"

"Yes. He hopes to leave on the eighteenth of May. I accompany him. We will probably stay in Hong Kong some days en route."

"Excellent. Excellent. Listen, tell him you will arrange the accommodation in Hong Kong. There is a *pensione* on Lantao island. I will give you details. He will certainly take the seed with him."

Their conversation was soon over. As the man made to get out, Irina said urgently: "Have you no news for me?"

"Not yet," said the man heavily.

"My father is still in prison?"

"Detained only."

Despite her efforts, her voice broke.

"He is over seventy!"

"Young enough still to do great harm. It is a very serious charge against him. You realise the full significance of what he was doing, do you not? He was attempting to carry out of Russia the manuscript of subversive literature, highly damaging to the Soviet Union."

"He did not know what was in the manuscript."

"This is not credible. He was the friend of the author."

"He could not have known he was doing anything wrong. He went on holiday only. Only to see me and also his brother after twenty years. His brother in Paris. Before they both die. He is not trying to do anything." Irina's voice was rising.

"Control yourself. Your father will be released soon if you help us sufficiently. There is no cause for alarm. These things take time. When I have details of your accommodation in Hong Kong, I will let you know."

He opened the door and disappeared. Irina saw the headlamps of the Fiat sway and the car flee into the night. She sat for some moments without moving, staring sightlessly out at the dark street. Finally, she let in the clutch and drew out from the kerb. The MG roared away, in a few seconds attaining a speed rarely seen on Mort Street.

# CHAPTER ELEVEN

"SO YOU FOUND CHARLIE?" Duquesne demanded of Street in the bar at Lakeside later that Thursday evening.

"Eh? Oh, yes. Yes, I found him." Street jumped up from a big leather armchair, his repose shattered. "What'll you have?" He beckoned to the waiter. "I half-wish I hadn't."

"How so?"

Street turned to Duquesne, seriousness taking possession of his face. "He's a very unhappy man, whose conscience is troubling him. He feels he deserted you and that the work was so important he should have made a stand."

"Go on."

"Charlie was hustled out of Ranger," Street continued very quietly. "Almost overnight."

"Why?"

"Robertson killed a man. Charlie saw it. Robertson made him help bury him. Charlie was paid not to talk. But there was more to it than that."

Duquesne started.

"Good God. The poor old devil."

Both were suddenly aware of a third man approaching. Tall and sparely built, with untidy black hair, his keen eyes regarded them pleasantly from behind rimless spectacles.

Street got up abruptly and said: "Well met. Meet Dr. Duquesne. This is Professor Woods, Duquesne, whom you know about."

"Pleased to meet you, Dr. Duquesne." Woods's voice, soft now, had the range and easy accents of the lecturer. He gripped Duquesne's hand firmly. "Tell me, is our meeting feasible? I'm free tomorrow night. Could we have dinner together?"

Thinking of Dick, whom he had promised to dine with, Duquesne said: "I could probably make tomorrow night. Would you like to meet me at the Singapore in Manuka? I can recommend their food. I could book a table."

"Splendid. For three, then? John Silkin here is my collaborator on the book, as you know."

"I didn't." Duquesne looked at Street. "I thought," he said deliberately, "that he was an insurance agent."

Woods looked puzzled, then laughed and gave a comical grimace, slapping Street on the back. "Journalists have their ways! I've got to hurry."

Duquesne waited until Woods's tall figure had disappeared before he rounded on Street.

"What *is* your name? And who the hell are you anyway?"

His companion took a card out of his wallet and gave it to Duquesne. It said: "John Silkin, Journalist. *Newslook.*"

"Then, why the devil do you call yourself Street?"

His face working, Silkin said: "Sorry about that. You know how lots of people feel about reporters. I thought it better to keep the paper out of it, especially as Charlie has nothing to do with my job."

"I don't understand you. Who did Robertson kill?" asked Duquesne roughly, cutting through the other's words.

"Someone trying to steal some plants. He didn't succeed." Silkin stared at Duquesne. "You didn't hear of it?"

"No, I didn't." Duquesne's hand suddenly shot out, and he gripped Silkin's arm. "Who was it after the plants?"

Silkin looked alarmed and licked his lips.

"I can't tell you that. Er, have you ever considered—of course you *have*—who would most benefit from such a—what shall I call it?—well, something so very useful as was growing there? Or, on the other hand, what interests might be most damaged by the er . . . full-scale utilisation?"

Duquesne's hand dropped, and Silkin backed hurriedly away, turning on his heel.

"Till tomorrow night." With a half-salute, he hurried off across the carpeted expanse.

Duquesne remained where he was for some time, angry and worried. Then he called Dick from a phonebox in the lobby.

"I'll have to break our date for dinner tomorrow night. I have to meet a couple of chaps for a talk about shop. Tomorrow is the only time this bigwig can make it."

"That's all right. I presume our little jaunt still stands for Saturday."

"Oh, yes. Sorry about tomorrow. I'll take them to the Singapore anyway. It's the best food in Canberra."

Duquesne felt awkward and wondered if Dick were thinking of going on his own.

"I'll probably have a prime steak at home, then."

Due to spend Friday at an experimental station outside of Canberra, Duquesne got back late to the office, hoping to have a talk with Beattie or Sir John, but they had already left.

He cleared his desk, leaving the in-tray, with two new memoranda in it, till last.

The first memorandum raised a point which could be clarified by a call to Dobbs, a colleague at the CSIRO experimental farm at Katherine. On an impulse Duquesne put through a call at once and found Dobbs in.

After they had settled the matter in hand, Duquesne asked about the wheat plants.

"Most of those saved from the fire are doing well. We've had them in the ground sixteen—no, seventeen days, counting the Monday itself."

"Monday?" Duquesne glanced at a calendar. "You got them Monday?"

"Yes, Monday the twenty-first." Dobbs was quite definite. "Barry brought them along on the Monday-morning routine run down here."

They talked for a little longer before Duquesne rang off. He sat for some minutes before dialling the Lakeside Hotel. It took them a little while to locate Silkin. With a cold finger at his heart, Duquesne heard Silkin confirm the date of the fire. The fire had occurred on the evening of Tuesday the 22nd. The plants, ostensibly saved from the fire, had actually been sent down to Dobbs the morning of the day before. There could be no doubt. The fire had been deliberate.

Duquesne rose slowly and automatically put his desk in order. The other memorandum still lay in the in-tray, and his eyes ran over it. It bore that day's date, was signed Beattie and informed Duquesne that "owing to unavoidable pressure of work" his application for special leave to attend the FAO conference on grains had, unfortunately, to be refused.

Duquesne's actions in the next few moments lacked logical sequence. He picked up a pen, doodled on the desk, threw the pen down, made for the door and slammed it behind him. Halfway down the corridor he went back to his office and locked up his papers. He removed his spectacles and passed a weary hand across his eyes. They were burning. Finally he flung himself from the room as if unseen hands propelled him.

The evening at the Singapore had to be got through. The traffic was sparse, and Duquesne found himself at the restaurant ten minutes early, so he asked for his table and ordered a whisky. It was a good table, set comfortably in a corner against a wooden latticework of elaborate Indonesian carving which divided the restaurant in two.

Woods and Silkin were not long in coming. Duquesne watched them walk in—Silkin, with his usual compound of nonchalance and shabbiness, following slightly behind Woods, dressed casually but with an air of unmistakable distinction. Duquesne surprised in himself a vague hostility. Was it the assurance of Woods, which seemed to imply a superior understanding of the frailties and doubts of other men? Woods's reputation was well known to him, of course: a man of impeccable scholarship and great intellectual vigour—a well-known author and left-wing sympathiser, who had been active in the practical business of advising the Labour movement as to its foreign policy in the Pacific basin. His role in converting the Labour Party to establishing links between Australia and China was one of his recent achievements. A good man. But Duquesne still sensed a hostility in himself.

"Dr. Duquesne, I must apologise for allowing you to arrive first," said Woods, smiling warmly.

"It's no matter at all," Duquesne answered. "I filled in the time most satisfactorily." He waved at his glass.

"Then, we will all have a fill of satisfaction," said Silkin immediately, ordering three whiskies.

Afterwards, it seemed as if it was one of those dinners destined to become alcoholic. Silkin drank on Woods's money, Duquesne drank to bury his worries and his reaction to Woods, and Woods seemed happy to nurse his glass. Duquesne also realised he had been questioned deftly and thoroughly about the things Woods wanted to know. He was primarily interested in Duquesne's firsthand experience in plant breeding and introduction in Indonesia and the Philippines, where he had worked on rice and pulses. Duquesne found himself reliving those immensely satisfying years again. He described his work at the research institutes, the excitement at the first evidence of success—of significant improvements in yields or of disease resistance. He recalled the long hours in the laboratory and the experimental plots, the lively parties and the beautiful, delicately formed Asian girls, characterised by physical grace and remarkably few inhibitions. He described with feeling working with extension staff, patiently explaining the advantages of the new seeds to sceptical farmers who knew only too well that if they depended on these new seeds and the crop failed it would be their families who would suffer. The educated advisers would still get their salaries and live in big houses, but the moneylenders would impose even harsher terms on the farmers.

"And they were right to be so sceptical, wouldn't you say?" Woods wondered aloud as Duquesne fell into silent reverie.

"God, yes. Of course. They remembered only too well how many times they had been given bloody silly advice by city types who visited the farm once and then went away."

"But it was different, the way your extension teams worked?" asked Woods.

Duquesne explained how he and his people selected one district and lived there in their caravans, spending every day with the farmers, especially prior to the planting season, when decisions were being made. They were present when farmers were visited by the co-operative or the local representative of the Rural Bank to negotiate credit for purchasing seeds and fertiliser. They intervened in the haggling with merchants. Gradually they gained the confidence of farmers, and gradually more farmers turned to the new seeds and went into debt to buy the additional fertiliser, the additional water needed.

Woods was impressed.

"I didn't know you were an applied man also. I thought you were the pure scientist," he said. "Actually, you have given me a more vivid picture of what is involved in boosting food production than I've ever had. I'm very grateful. My book must get the balance between potentialities, constraints and the pace of adoption of new technologies absolutely right. I'm particularly interested in the repercussions there could be on the pattern of international power of either an acceleration or a slowing down of the trend of food production."

Duquesne felt his earlier hostility had gone. Woods was a good man. He told Silkin so, while Woods was out in the lobby telephoning.

"Woods is a goods man."

Silkin laughed. He proposed they should top off the evening with a bottle of champagne. Duquesne was happy with the suggestion. He had no one to go home to and he enjoyed talking to his host.

"One of the splendid things about being a scientist is that one is so completely spared any direct involvement in the political dimensions of the problem," Woods was saying a little later, choosing his words delicately and perhaps provocatively.

Duquesne felt a surge of bitterness rising.

"Yes," he said. "That's the conventional wisdom. Society leaves the scientist to work in his ivory tower and never is the lucky fellow interfered with. It's nonsense. Sheer bloody nonsense."

He was talking too loudly and too emphatically, but it didn't matter.

"Do you really mean that, Dr. Duquesne?" Woods asked in surprise, and Duquesne noticed for a fleeting second how intently Silkin, all drunkenness gone, was watching the two of them.

"Certainly I do. Political power, bureaucratic power—they are both encroaching steadily on the prerogatives that the discipline of science demands. It must be resisted, I tell you. It's not new. Galileo knew what interference meant. And you probably remember Oppenheimer, the American who worked on the atomic bomb. A brilliant man. A senior scientist. And what happened to him?" Duquesne paused for dramatic effect. Really, he was himself quite an actor, he decided. But it was wrong that Woods, an eminent man, to whom the nation listened, should not know the realities.

"Yes, I recall that he fell out of favour," Woods replied quietly to the question which Duquesne had every intention of answering himself.

" 'Fell out of favour'! The bastards in Washington got him removed from his job, even had him denied access to the results of his own work, ruined his career and his health. And all because he was supposed to be a communist or a communist sympathiser. As though that mattered!"

"But that was some time ago," commented Silkin. "Surely such a thing couldn't happen now. No scientist could be gagged for such a reason now."

"How do you know?" demanded Duquesne belligerently, leaning over the table towards Silkin, who hastily pushed his chair back. "I tell you," he went on, "there are things being done now that you don't know about. How can you? Only if the scientists concerned are prepared to damn themselves, forget Official Secrets Acts and all that kind of bilge. I tell you, more and more I am coming to believe they should put their loyalty to their discipline first and to their country only second."

"Indeed, it isn't difficult to comprehend the attitudes of the scientist." Woods's voice fell like honey on the turbulence of Duquesne's tirade. "You're probably damned glad, Duquesne, you're a plant scientist and as such removed from such terrible questions."

" 'Removed.' That's good, that's really good." Duquesne laughed, slapping the table forcefully. "Oh God, that's good."

"The underlying questions are very complex in these matters," said Woods quietly, "too much so for a historian like myself to understand."

Duquesne stared at him.

"Too complex for a historian like yourself? *You*—unable to understand—after that book . . ." His voice became vague, and he found he could not remember, suddenly, what anyone had been saying. Silkin's face was close, and he was pouring a drink. Then, remarkably, he and Woods were alone, and Silkin had disappeared.

"Have you seen . . . seen . . . ?" Duquesne gestured largely.

"He'll be back in a moment. Look, what you've been telling me", Woods was saying, "has been nothing short of fascinating, and most germane to the subject of my book."

Then Woods was paying the bill and Silkin was suddenly back, and hurrying Woods up. Silkin's voice was urgent.

Duquesne remembered then what it was he had to tell them.

" 'Member that book now—about Sukarno. You . . ." Only then he lost it again.

He was walking out with Woods and Silkin and—most unaccountably—he was sitting beside Silkin in his own Alfa, while Silkin drove it. Then, somehow, he was in bed, and saying to Silkin: "You're a good chap, Street, only you're not Street, are you? Damned nice. And Woods is goods! Damned nice dinner, too."

# CHAPTER TWELVE

DUQUESNE SAT in the switching sunlight that bore through the windows of Dick Temple's Volkswagen. Conversation was uneven, limp on Duquesne's side, persistent on Dick's.

Duquesne's drunkenness had sent him into a stupor from which a telephone call from Dick had awakened him at eight, and only a parched feeling now remained. On his insistence, they stopped for a beer at Bungendore, and the beer made Duquesne lightheaded. He could even—wryly—smile now at his situation. His fury over the deliberate burning of the wheat and the refusal to grant him leave, his uneasy recollection of his unguarded vehemence over dinner last night had receded a little. He found that he had already reached a decision. The repressive measures against him had become intolerable. The refusal of his leave he saw as the last humiliation in a chain of humiliations, and the most cruel and damaging. And unnecessary —unless they considered him untrustworthy.

Part of his anger stemmed from thoughts of shame before Irina. She wanted so much to go to Rome with him. But, if he accepted the decision about his leave, they wouldn't be going.

"That man Harding with the shop at Manly. Oh, he's good. I ordered that underwater suit a fortnight ago and got it in no time."

Dick's breezy words swirled round Duquesne, and Duquesne was not displeased to be where he was this morning. He had a sense of freedom with Dick, who knew nothing of his personal or professional life and was moreover a foreigner in the country.

"A tailored suit, eh?" said Duquesne.

"Mmm? Oh, certainly!" A mighty chuckle shook Dick's huge frame. "I'm hardly stock size."

Duquesne, in a state of emotional arrest, was conscious of the big man's power as he watched the great arms, bare from the elbow, on the wheel. Dick handled the car like a toy.

"How have you solved your problem of vision underwater?" demanded Dick.

"Oh, I have a very fancy mask indeed with special lenses. Ron Harding fixed that, too."

"That must have cost you money."

"Well, either you see underwater or you're crazy if you go there."

Descending the Clyde, they were suddenly in the flat slower rhythm imposed by the clammy sea-air. Dick had brought food with him and would not let Duquesne stop for provisions in Batemans Bay. He joked: "Tonight we'll either eat the best the ocean has to offer or we make do with the best you've got on land."

He had brought two T-bone steaks of great size.

"It may not, of course, compare with your meal of last night at the Singapore," he added.

"Not as liquid a meal anyway," grunted Duquesne.

"Oh, are you fit to go down today? It's not to be recommended usually after a hangover."

"I'm all right."

"I was fearful for our expedition this morning. I wondered if your conference might carry over to the weekend or, more especially, if you might end by combining business with pleasure today."

"Bring 'em down here, you mean? Oh, no, indeed." Duquesne grinned. "Neither looked the athletic type."

"I can depend on it that neither will take your attention from more important fishing matters, then, for the course of the weekend?"

"I never even mentioned I was coming down here," said Duquesne in surprise. "In any case they are off to Sydney again this morning."

"I like to get off by myself, some place where no one can follow me," drawled Dick.

Duquesne thought of the regular-featured firm-lipped woman on top of Dick's piano.

"I always think of Rosedale as my safety-valve—my escape-hatch, if you like."

"So you didn't tell anyone you were coming down here today?"

"Eh? No, no one," said Duquesne absently.

"I wondered if they were old friends of yours, the two last night, turning up so suddenly."

"No." Duquesne's tone was dry. "One is a distinguished professor of history who wants to pick my brains for a book he's writing and the other is his rouseabout."

"Somehow not the most pleasing of sensations, having one's brains picked. The price to pay, I imagine, for being an eminent man in your field."

Duquesne laughed with sudden bitterness.

"Eminent! Eminent enough to be gagged and impeded at every step by the short-sighted bunch at the top in this country."

"You're kidding!" Dick was shocked. "This is Australia, not some socialist country."

"Australia Felix! Which nevertheless is these days pursuing a policy of gross self-interest and is indifferent to the sufferings of three-quarters of the world." Duquesne's words were deliberately enunciated.

"Why, Jack, you're a revolutionary this morning," drawled Dick. "In some places what you say would be dangerous words. And you're speaking of what will probably be my adopted country."

"You've left your own country, haven't you?" demanded Duquesne. "Isn't that an admission of dissatisfaction?"

"And you plan to leave yours, do you?"

Duquesne laughed, in a secret manner, as Dick parked the VW in the carport attached to the beach-house.

"You know, it wouldn't be utterly impossible."

And together they got out and walked to the edge of the cliff-face, over the sandy soil with its carpet of she-oak needles, and surveyed the hard glitter of the sea. Then they slid down the track to the beach and ploughed along by the foaming edge of the water.

"Not another soul in sight," said Dick. "That's one almighty privilege Australia can afford."

"Only at this time of the year. In summer there are people."

"Quite seriously, Jack, do you mean what you said back there about quitting this country?"

"This country and all its works. Christ, I never felt more serious." Duquesne picked up a flat stone and flicked it with such force that it skidded on the water half a dozen times before it was swallowed up.

Later, shining and black-skinned, a spurious sea-creature in that timeless other world of his, a seventy-pound bottle of air harnessed to his back, Duquesne moved slowly, with seemingly effortless strokes of his flippers, through the silent translucence, shedding worry as he had shed all sense of gravity, an exultant intruder thirty feet down in a country of pastel browns and greens, of pink and ochre rock, of emerald shot-silk waters, of tragic and sunken-eyed bejewelled forms, of undulating movement. Above Duquesne swam the huge shadowy figure of Dick. He had wanted them to use a "buddy-line," a common diving device, he said, in the States. Duquesne, who often went down alone, had demurred, with an instinctive dislike of such a safety measure.

It was Duquesne's sea, with its clarity and brightness this fine morning, and with pride he guided Dick to his most spectacular haunts, avoiding the slippery amber strands of seaweed, following the reefs. Fish were everywhere; blue-tailed whiting and colourful parrot fish in the seaweed, though their soft flesh had no attraction for Duquesne. Black and white cockies, sluggish scavengers, kept close to the rocks. All of a sudden an elegant trevally crossed their line of vision. Duquesne released his spear but missed the fish. He was not alert this morning. The trevally flicked itself clear and, with a graceful turn, disappeared. Valuable moments passed tracking a well-padded blue groper, three feet long, which kept just out of range of their spears until it came across a conveniently sized cave to foil them.

With his fingers Duquesne indicated they were going down to deeper water towards the bombora. As they approached, a yellow-tail kingfish circled around them, keeping well out of range. At what Duquesne's depth-gauge told him was fifty-five feet, the silver hues of fishes, the gorgeous colours of the rocks perceptibly faded. Colder silken hands caressed them.

There, by all things wonderful, was that fish so strangely named a boar fish, with its graceful veils of fins moving in harmony, perhaps the most elegant one of all in those waters.

And then, in some quiet water between the reefs, Duquesne saw a banded morwong—cream, brown and inquisitive. It turned side-on to inspect Duquesne, who did not miss this time. He transferred the fish from the barb of his spear to the wire line around his waist and glanced back at Dick. Dick was uncoiling his line from his waist. He must also have speared a fish. Duquesne looked at his watch. Twenty minutes to go before the bigger man's air gave out. Duquesne prepared to ascend and made a half-turn, pointing to his watch to let Dick know they should start back.

And, as he made this turn, the huge dark figure descended upon him. Slowly, Dick's arms passed round Duquesne's body in a wide embrace, and slowly withdrew.

What are you doing, for God's sake, Dick? Are you thinking of your buddy-line still? Have you mistaken me for a tunny? Duquesne's alarm mounted. His eyes spoke mutely behind the glass of his mask. Can't you *see* at this depth, Dick? Or are you so gauche, so crazy? Or are you ill? Go away, Dick. Go away.

Duquesne kicked helplessly, his movements slowed by the water, and was halted abruptly. A constricting band of pain in upper arms and chest led to the incredible discovery that his arms were now lashed to his sides. Unbelieving, he watched Dick knot the lasso.

All right, Dick, this is the biggest fool joke anyone can play down here. Now, hurry up and loose this bloody cord.

Through his mask Duquesne made a horrible grimace and thrashed hopelessly with his legs. Then, slowly and relentlessly, he found himself spun round, drawn backwards. What horrible indignity, to be brought thus helplessly towards his persecutor, who slowly, slowly, was paying in the line.

A bad joke, Dick. A most un-American, ungentlemanly joke, Dick —unless you're telling me my equipment's gone wrong. But why, then, in the name of Heaven, don't you lead me to the surface?

Duquesne sought helplessly for his knife. Strapped to his right calf, it was unobtainable. He kicked with his legs. Tried somersaulting. Each movement was a futile essay, horribly prolonged, rendered feeble by the pressure of water, straight away aborted.

Dick's hands were fumbling at Duquesne's mask. With a horror that tore at his bowels, Duquesne felt the icy touch of water on his face, and at the sight of the cold eyes regarding him knew he was to die.

"This is the right place, but Duquesne's not here at the moment."

Jerry Hill, crouched on Duquesne's doorstep at Hackett, blew the wood dust away from the hole he was drilling in the front door. His eyes left his Black & Decker only long enough to get a brief impression of a small man who looked white and anxious in the morning sunlight.

"His car's still here," said Silkin uneasily, a nerve twitching his eyelid.

Jerry set down his drill and got to his feet, pushing his lips slightly forward as he looked down on Silkin. With a shade of the bully in his slow deliberation, he took his time to concede this.

"When will he be back?" demanded Silkin desperately.

Jerry shrugged.

"I can't say. He's out of Canberra."

"What!"

Jerry looked Silkin over.

"Something eating you?"

"I saw him only hours ago. We spent the evening together. I brought him back here." Silkin thrust a business card at Jerry.

Jerry glanced at it and said: "He's gone down the coast."

"Without his car?"

"He's with another chap."

"Would the other man's wife know when they'll be back?"

"He doesn't seem to have one. He's an American—Duquesne's tenant actually."

Silkin moved convulsively. "An American! Not a . . . fat American?"

Jerry looked amused now.

"That's exactly how you'd describe him. A big fat American. They've gone fishing."

Silkin became paler still. He stood staring at Jerry. In the flat opposite a singer screamed: "I'm just sinkin' in an ocean of tee-ahs." A man was polishing his car further down the courtyard, and from a greater distance came the noise of a motor-mower.

A little boy came pedalling up on a tricycle and chanted to Jerry: "*You* don't live *here!*"

Jerry looked round and said, "That's right, Buster," and grimaced horribly, and the child squealed and pedalled away.

Into this normality, Silkin dropped the incongruous words: "Duquesne's life is in danger."

Jerry set the Black & Decker down gently on the linoleum inside the front door and told Silkin to come in the house.

"You know this place they've gone to?" Silkin stepped inside.

Jerry nodded.

"Can you drive me down there? Now?"

Silkin's degree of urgency was a force in itself, and was finally having a hypnotic effect on Jerry, who motioned him to a chair and said: "All right. Talk, Mr. Silkin."

Silkin replied, with such vehemence that Jerry was impressed even further: "I could tell you as we drive. It's big stuff, and it's complicated, and it has to do with Duquesne's work and all sorts of things. We'd waste an hour."

Jerry, with a slightly ugly expression on his face, said: "Get in the car, Mr. Silkin. It's the station-wagon out there. You can talk as we go."

Duquesne wanted to struggle, to fight, to shout at Dick, to grind that intent face to a pulp. If only he could get his knife to Dick's throat. . . . But he was trussed like a chicken, doubly a prisoner of Dick and of the impotence imposed by this hostile element. And Dick—an instrument of torture, cold-blooded as a fish—was removing Duquesne's mask.

Scraps of his old diving manual came back to Duquesne. "If your bottle cuts out, it is easy to surface. You pout your lips and let air escape in small bubbles, which you follow to the surface." But Dick would hold him there, clearly enough—hold him until water burst his lungs, roared in his ears, flooded his brain, left him swollen flotsam.

He could no longer reason. There were two Dicks now anyway. Too many Dicks. Another Dick was beside the first, another black-suited Dick. The other head of this two-headed monster. Only it did not seem to be Dick. It seemed, crazily, to be Jerry. Only it was of course Dick, and there was Dick's intent face close to him.

Then suddenly Dick's hands fell away and at the same time he went backwards, his eyeballs showing. Dick was floundering, feet waving. And then came Jerry in his place, and Jerry was busy with his knife, cutting through Duquesne's bonds, and then, moving with the languor dictated by the sea, yet conveying urgency, Jerry was twisting, gliding off to where—was it possible?—a burst of ascending bubbles preceded monster Dick's slow, slow, upward thrust towards the surface.

Christ, I'll kill you, Dick, if I can. I'll kill you, Dick, if you're not already dead, or is that a trick? Not too close. You're struggling, aren't you? Jerry's cut your breathing tube. Which is lucky, Dick, because I haven't much strength left, thanks to you.

You bloody bastard. Attack me, would you? Oh God. . . .

And Duquesne, a concentration of white rage, slid slowly, slowly, purposefully, after Jerry, after the great uncertain body of Dick, and then they were both grasping Dick. Then all was a terrible confusion of black slow-flailing bodies as they fought to hold Dick fast, to hold him fast in the water, until the powerful resistance of the huge body gradually lessened, the legs and arms became still, and—finally—the bubbles stopped coming.

# CHAPTER THIRTEEN

JERRY WAS THE FIRST TO SURFACE. He dragged his share of Dick's gear up on the beach and helped Duquesne to dry land. When he stripped off his mask, Duquesne trembled uncontrollably. He sat there and struggled, gasping in the sweet air, his eyes half-closed against the sun.

"Why? Why me? Why try to kill me?"

"To stop you talking."

"What?"

"You were sounding off last night over dinner—about interference in your work."

The cold douche of this information stopped Duquesne's writhing.

"Dick was in the Singapore," Jerry went on. "Silkin saw him."

"How did you know all this?" Duquesne demanded.

"Silkin. He made me come down here."

The sun was high now, resplendent. Jerry's glance took in the lazy incessant rollers, the curve of the deserted beach.

"We'd better get up to the house. Can you make it?"

Slowly they started up the steep track.

Duquesne stopped halfway up to look at Jerry with horror.

"There wasn't any other way out. I had to kill him after he tried to murder me."

"We'd better get under cover." Jerry was inexorable, his hand gripping Duquesne's arm. "Silkin'll be up there."

"How did you time it like that? Thank God you did!"

"We watched you and Temple go down. I had my suit and gear with me. My idea had been to arrive here as though I was suddenly fed up and wanted to go fishing. Break in on your weekend. When we saw you going under so soon, I simply followed as quickly as I could."

"Where the hell *is* Silkin?"

The house was completely quiet, as though waiting. Jerry put on a kettle, then they went outside to strip off their suits.

"You haven't told me why yet—why Temple was out for me," said Duquesne.

Jerry, a handsome buccaneer in his black skin-tight suit, against the backdrop of limitless blue, paused in the act of unzipping his jacket. The sun picked out every pugnacious line on his face, which was older now, and concerned.

"He's CIA. According to Silkin, the top man in Australia. . . ."

There was a rustling, and from the tangled bush above appeared a distraught white face.

"Where is he?"

"In a cave," Jerry said brutally. "Seventy feet down."

Silkin came down, breathing hard. Duquesne, in a dream, saw that Silkin's teeth were really chattering.

"He won't trouble you again," said Jerry. "But remember, you're now an accessory."

Silkin looked fearfully at the suit and bottle on the ground.

"You're sure there's nothing left to identify him?"

"We stripped him clean up on the reef."

Silkin jumped.

"Was that wise? Someone could have seen you."

"We had no alternative. We were getting short of air by then."

Inside they drank tea, then whisky. Duquesne was still dazed. He had to rethink, recreate Dick Temple, who had become a friend. Admittedly, the hard core of Dick had been unknown, but the veneer had been likeable. When the alcohol began to settle him, Duquesne turned to Silkin.

"How long have you known Temple was a CIA man?" he asked him roughly.

"Quite a while." Silkin was evasive.

Duquesne said, suddenly furious: "By God, you could have saved me all this. You knew and yet you never told me!"

Silkin jumped up and retreated.

"Wait a minute! You wouldn't have believed me."

"What evidence have you that he was CIA?"

Silkin glanced quickly at him and said: "Journalists pick things up. I can't give you tangible proof."

"Then, what non-tangible proof can you give me?"

Silkin grimaced.

"There's no doubt of it. He approached me to gather information for him."

"And you accepted?"

"What do you take me for?"

"It might be better," said Duquesne cruelly, "not to mention what I take you for. Of course it was quite at random that you were nosing round the trial crop at Ranger; it was quite at random you went after Charlie!"

"I smelt a story. . . ."

Duquesne rose abruptly.

"You know so damn much, Silkin," he shouted. "You know so damn much. How about just telling us the whole thing!"

Silkin paled and said: "Some might say I've . . . saved your life."

"By God . . . and d'you know what I say? I say that I've killed a man, and that's a capital crime, and if you'd had any decency you'd have warned me he was out to get me and I mightn't bloody well have had to do it."

Duquesne subsided, shaking.

Jerry growled at Silkin. "Get on with it," he ordered. "The lot. Everything you found out while you *weren't* working for the CIA."

Silkin's eyes slid from them and back, wavered, and he said, his formal tones now greatly exaggerated: "I was asked to get seed, wheat seed, under cover of an article I was doing on uranium mining."

"And did you?"

"I couldn't get near it. So the Americans sent in a helicopter to try to get plants. Robertson shot one of the men. Charlie saw it. Robertson made him help to bury the body. And he hustled Charlie out of camp very early the next morning. Charlie was offered a hundred and fifty thousand dollars in cash to stay out and shut up."

"Robertson offered him money like that?"

"Robertson acting for the Government. Quite suddenly," continued Silkin, "Temple's orders changed. First he wanted wheat samples. Then, overnight, things were turned back to front. I was warned off.

Then the wheat was burned. Temple gave me other jobs, but not on the wheat."

"Why would they lose interest at that point?"

"I think because they already had the information by other means. Because they'd got what they wanted—suppression of the wheat. One night I had to go to Temple's flat in Sydney. He let me in and said he had to finish a private telephone call. But I went to the door of the room where he was talking. It was just a bit ill-fitting. I could hear what he said. He referred to uranium and then I heard your name, Duquesne. You were somehow linked with uranium."

"Uranium. . . ." Duquesne was feeling cold, despite the alcohol, and finding it hard to follow Silkin.

"I think a bargain was struck," said Silkin. "Australia's suppression of your wheat, in return for a contract of great benefit to the Australian uranium industry. A week ago the Government announced it had decided to permit the mining and export of uranium. At the same time it was announced that America had contracted to take the total output of Ranger's uranium—the most binding and long-term business agreement the two countries have ever made."

"But you don't have tangible proof. It's only what you've pieced together yourself," said Jerry sternly.

"Temple was out to silence me from the beginning, and was ready to kill if he thought it better," said Duquesne. He was quieter now, overcome with a terrible weariness.

"Only if you talked too much."

"And I did just that last night, didn't I, with Woods?"

"Yes, you did just that," agreed Silkin. "I didn't see Temple until it was too late. I won't easily forget the moment I clapped eyes on that great fat back of his. I was coming back from the washroom. There he was, sitting by himself on the other side of that dividing screen in the restaurant. He heard everything."

Duquesne had subsided, slouched in his chair.

"What now?" he asked. "He's out of the way. Snug and safe in the reefs, with a nice big stone in front of the cave to keep him there."

Silkin's eyes shifted uneasily.

"Aren't there lots of skin divers around these days?"

"Novices mostly," said Jerry. "Not likely to be snooping round at sixty or seventy feet down. It's pretty dark in the reefs—all dark rock and hardly any colour left. Temple's in a cave that a skin diver couldn't easily enter. Maybe a fifty-pound groper could get in."

"Or a shark?" asked Silkin nervously.

"Sharks are fussy—or frightened—in the reef country close to shore. But the odd old shark would wander in if the tidewater was warm enough."

Silkin shuddered, and Jerry followed up his advantage by adding cruelly: "I wonder if Temple had a cobber who knows about you, Silkin?"

"I'm small fry," said Silkin, bracing himself. "But there is Temple's car and his suit and bottle to be disposed of. And what happens when he fails to turn up in Canberra?"

Duquesne was silent, still slumped in his chair, working things over.

"The car might be picked up very soon if it's abandoned on the road, or even in the bush," said Silkin. "The city would be worse."

"It would be safest to put the car back in your own garage in Forrest," said Jerry, "together with the suit and bottle. Does anyone else know you came down here with him today, Jack?"

Duquesne shook his head. "No one." Then he remembered Irina. He repeated: "No one."

"Did you speak to anyone on the way down? When you put in for petrol, for instance?"

Duquesne didn't take the question in at first.

"We stopped for a beer at Bungendore," he said finally. "That's right. He didn't want to. I insisted. I had a huge thirst. He stayed in the car. He wouldn't let me stop for food later on. He said he'd bought all we needed. He had, too." He added, half-wonderingly: "We didn't stop for petrol, either. He had it all made."

"Didn't you stop for compressed air?"

"No. My bottle was full, and his had been filled when he got it."

"See anyone you know as you came through Batemans and along this road?"

"Not a soul."

"Did you speak to anyone when you left Hackett this morning, or did anyone see you go off with him?"

Duquesne said: "He telephoned early and said he was coming over at nine, as we'd agreed. He said he would stop in the road and I was to come out. Nobody saw us leave."

"You'd better not be seen driving his car," said Jerry. "I'll drive it back to Canberra myself. I'll wait until midnight or later to garage it."

"All right. I'll take yours, then," agreed Duquesne.

"Sure you are fit enough, Jack?" asked Jerry, who had taken command.

"I am. What about his lifeline? It's been cut."

"I'll substitute mine for his," said Jerry immediately. "Mine came from Ron Harding as well. There shouldn't be a thing left to connect him with Rosedale."

"Please God," put in Silkin prayerfully.

With urgent care they removed all trace of their brief stay, stowing all Dick's provisions in his car once more. Dick's diving suit followed, and his bottle.

They checked the car for further trace of Dick's activities, but found nothing, except that under the dashboard, neatly attached by a magnet, was a gleaming little Mauser. Jerry said that a Smith & Wesson would have been more in order.

Silkin drove and Duquesne slept, exhausted. When finally he awoke, it was to darkness and the brilliance of headlamps and the rush of cool night air. Silkin drew to the side of the road and poured hot tea from a Thermos, and Duquesne roused himself. All at once he was talking with nervous impatience.

"You're not sorry, are you, Silkin, that he's out of the way?"

"No more than you are, Duquesne."

"Christ! I—we talked. We talked—about all sorts of things. Not wheat, you understand."

"All right. I believe you."

"But we talked a hell of a lot, about everything." Duquesne wandered for a moment, then said bitterly: "I trusted the man. I liked him. I felt—safe with him. I mean, for me he was simply an American who wanted a house to rent and get away from his wife for a while. He even installed a dishwasher, d'you know? For his wife. Her photo was up on the piano. She probably doesn't even exist."

"Did he talk about himself?"

"God, yes. I can see now he was acting a perfect part, because that way he wormed himself into my confidence. It was masterly. He didn't seem to ask questions—he talked about himself. But somehow you found yourself talking about the things that you felt most strongly about. He seemed a lonely sort of blighter. He was so obviously a failure in his own country. More than once he referred to people who'd let him down—people of his own class. Because he was very much upper class. Of course, he was testing me out."

"Exactly. But at the same time he was both a member of the entrenched and moneyed upper class and"—Silkin's voice shook—"an utterly cold and arrogant member, who treated his inferiors like dirt—or those whom he paid." Resentment spilled out from Silkin.

"Yes," said Duquesne vaguely. In his state it was hard to concentrate for long. "What a story. The story you were out to get. But you can't use it now."

"I might have wanted a story at the beginning. I want something more now. A political explosion."

"Oh!" Duquesne came to life. "A political explosion! Is Woods in this, by any chance? Nuclear energy for the rich before bread for the poor. Biggest thing ever." Duquesne laughed wildly. "A dangerous game, Silkin. You need evidence. You need witnesses. But a man's been killed now—another man—and that changes things. I've been tricked and spied on and impeded. I've had my work thrown back in my face. I've just escaped death. . . ."

Suddenly, behind his torment, behind the black veil of his despair, a healthier, vigorous anger was kindled in Duquesne, and a final decision was quickly taken.

"I'm getting out," he declared.

"Out of Canberra?"

"Out of Australia. I've even the occasion to do so. There's a UN conference in Italy that I've been invited to." His voice went hard. "And I've been forbidden to attend it."

Silkin said thoughtfully: "Can you go, then, if CSIRO doesn't allow it?"

"I was invited in a private capacity, not as a member of CSIRO. I can take leave. I'm overdue, as it happens, and I forfeit it otherwise. They can't stop it. They needn't even know."

"It's probably a good thing, short of putting you in cottonwool for a while, Duquesne."

"I've been victimised enough and I'm not going to be used any longer as a pawn in this bloody political game." Duquesne was hard and definite.

And the station-wagon, which had slowed under the impact on Silkin of this declaration, picked up speed again and thrust into the night.

# PART TWO

# FERTILE GROUND

# CHAPTER ONE

A WEEK LATER, Duquesne was in Sydney. Without demur, CSIRO had granted him two weeks' leave. But it did not take in the FAO conference period.

"You understand, Jack," Beattie had said, "the situation is delicate. We think it would be easier for you, in the circumstances, not to attend."

"Much easier," agreed Duquesne pleasantly. "You'll notice I'm due back the day the Rome conference begins."

Though temporary flight from Australia was no real solution to anything, he ached to get away. It might also banish his recurring nightmare of a large white body gently waving in its underwater prison.

In Forrest not a soul had enquired for Dick, nor had any letters come for him. Duquesne and Jerry had searched the house, but found nothing which showed Dick to have been anything but a private American citizen. Silkin had taken possession of several sets of keys, one of which he found belonged to Dick's Sydney flat. But this flat, too, had revealed nothing of value to them.

Jerry had been Duquesne's mainstay since Dick's death. In the midst of his turmoil, Duquesne was moved by that rock-like devotion. Jerry, capable of efficient dishonesties, great and small, in business, had not only saved his life but also unhesitatingly taken command afterwards.

Walking into the international terminal at Sydney Airport Duquesne deposited his bags and went outside again. He had come to Sydney a day early to see his wife, to whom he had related everything, except for Irina. She had looked at him with wide frightened eyes across the barrier that separated them.

"I'm up to my neck," said Duquesne, "and I don't know what the devil I'll do. I've transferred all our savings to your account here and I've instructed the lawyer that in the event of my—non-return he is to put the Forrest house up for sale. . . ."

Meg had taken it as she took everything, with the dogged endurance so little indicated by her hesitant speech and awkward manner. He so admired her now he wondered how he had ever come near to hating her, when she had forced him back to Australia. Looking at her now, he saw the quick sympathy well up in her eyes as she gravely listened to his story. With no facility for words at all, she simply said: "If I can ever do anything, let me know, Jack."

Standing in the bright sunlight outside the international terminal building he watched Irina, the solitary passenger, climb from the little bus which had brought her from the TAA terminal. The driver swung himself down with alacrity to get her bags out, and Duquesne heard him say: "Have a good trip, miss. I'd take your bags in myself, but there'd be a rumpus. The bloke over there in the peaked cap will help you with them—hey, Joe!—in a manner of speaking."

His badinage reflected the light and sun and lazy good humour of Sydney. Irina was smiling at him.

Duquesne, slightly annoyed, came up behind her and said: "I'll take care of them."

She swung round, looking so radiant at the sight of him that his heart leaped. Outside were all the others.

Inside the terminal the clerk at the Cathay Pacific desk took their tickets and weighed bags. Duquesne paid their forty-dollar embarkation fees, and in a moment they were through.

Irina's eyes slid round.

"I'm nervous. I want something to steady me."

"Nothing simpler. We'll go to the bar."

Round them noise swirled. The air rang suddenly.

In the bar Duquesne found a couple of stools and a minute table and they raised glasses, regarding each other over the rims. He sat there admiring her. She looked superb in sea-green.

*"Salute!"* She smiled, and in two gulps emptied her glass.

Suddenly, he felt carefree; he had shrugged off the bonds of official Canberra.

"We'll lie in the sun in Hong Kong. By God, I hope your Lantao place cooks well, Irina. We'll lie in the sun and swim."

Her finely modelled lips trembled, and suddenly the quizzical smile was gone. He was puzzled to see her eyes were misty.

"Oh, they cook fine. Just fine."

"What's wrong?"

"Nothing's wrong, of course nothing's wrong. I'm . . . excited. I got up at five." She tossed her head and plonked her empty glass on the table. "Let's have another."

Carrying more drinks over, he thought she drank a lot now. He had seen her several times in the last few days, and she had twice drunk with a reckless gaiety enough to put most women—or men—under the table. But she had a good head for drink.

The voices around were raucous and the air full of cheerios and loud laughter.

"That's enough now," said Duquesne firmly. "Now we've got to go, Irina. Hell, we'll miss our plane."

He slid an arm round her and pushed her gently out, carrying in his other hand their two cabin-bags.

Outside the bar she turned suddenly to him, put one hand on his chest and in a husky voice said: "Jack, with all my heart, I want things to be well for you. With all my heart."

Her eyes held his insistently in a long moment. He laughed, a little awkwardly, but her eyes brushed the laugh aside and his own hand closed on hers.

"You darling," he murmured.

Then with one accord they walked together to the final checkpoint, across the long hall.

Standing in the queue, she said brightly: "Of course you are right, Jack. I want to do shopping in Hong Kong. I want to buy a . . . a screen. You get them so lovely there, Jack." Her hand inside his elbow gripped caressingly. "Lovely wood they have. I want a camphorwood chest, Jack, and some silk. I might get a fur."

She was chattering. He had never heard her chatter before. She talked insistently, the slightest bit hampered by the language. They laid their passports down on the desk together, and the stolid official behind the desk glanced at Duquesne's and said, "Holiday, is it, sir?"

and pushed it straight back. Irina's was given the same brief treatment, except that the man inspected her photograph with a little smile, and with a quirk of the mouth turned his eyes on her face, saying, with his eyes: "*That* doesn't do you justice." Men would always want to joke with Irina.

But Duquesne was appalled to see the pallor of her face. Then she appeared to relax, and the colour began to return. She grasped his arm hard. Just then the announcement came that flight CX100 was boarding, and they were swallowed up in the throng of passengers waiting to go through the metal detector. And now Irina was silent.

# CHAPTER TWO

THE DC10 THUNDERED up into the crystal sky, tracing a great arc over Botany Bay. Far below the white wash of the surf curved and curled around Maroubra, Coogee and Bondi, before the plane quivered and levelled over Port Jackson, giving its passengers a view of the Harbour Bridge. Duquesne, gazing down at the North Shore, wondered if his daughter Jane could hear the plane and what she was doing, with a mouth a little too tight-lipped, her eyes bright and watchful. He had told her only that he had had to go on a trip for a while. His heart went down to her in such a rush of feeling that his face paled, and Irina, still as a statue beside him, glanced sideways enquiringly.

The plane left behind the glistening indentations of Middle Harbour, abandoning—far to the right—the creamy wash where the turquoise-stained waters met the golden sands of Curl Curl and Dee Why, before it turned its nose inland.

"Irina, are you nervous of air travel? You are so tense."

Duquesne realised that they had never flown together before.

Irina put her hands over her eyes. Then her hands dropped.

"Perhaps I am nervous, Jack." And Duquesne sensed the suppressed sigh.

The No Smoking sign went off, then the seat-belts sign, and a pretty Asian stewardess tripped down the aisle to the front of the plane. Another rolled a drinks-trolley down from the back. Automatically they ordered Scotch, and Irina, tossing half hers down in reckless style, said: "To our very bon voyage."

In the brilliant light of upper air her skin was transparently faultless. Duquesne, smiling into her eyes, felt a vast calm creep over him. He took out a bundle of maps from his briefcase and said: "We'll do a little planning. We'll go to the Peak tomorrow, if we feel like it. It's

May and summer again in Hong Kong. We could go in late afternoon and come down on the cable car in the dark to see the lights. We can go to Cat Street first and look at the stalls and shops, if it's still the same, and that temple. Those streets, running up and down the hill-side. . . ."

Irina was recovering from her nervousness. She lay with her head back, watching him through half-closed lids, clasping his hand under cover of the tourist pamphlets.

"In the evening we'll eat at Swee Kee in Stanley Street and go back by the last boat to Lantao."

It was a direct flight. An hour after take-off they were served a wine-laden meal, and they dozed alternately or chatted, while the sky turned pink and they rushed into late afternoon.

Duquesne awoke to find the stewardess bent over him. She inclined her richly dressed hairdo and whispered.

"Eh? What? Not really? All right. . . ." Duquesne uncoiled himself and clambered to his feet. Irina was asleep, sprawled in an elegant diagonal. Duquesne straightened his jacket and followed the girl up the plane to the front.

On the flight deck the captain shook his hand and said briskly: "Ah, yes, Dr. Duquesne." He had a dark young face, a tight jaw.

Duquesne, still drowsy, stared at a myriad dials and controls.

"We're beyond Australia?" he asked, glimpsing patches of grey-blue forest through snowy swansdown.

"Getting towards the Philippines, Mindanao," said the pilot crisply. Duquesne thought he sounded like a New Zealander. He was quite young, in his thirties. He watched Duquesne with a worried expression.

"I've been requested to return to Darwin and set you down there."

The words came out so flat, so tonelessly, that Duquesne could hardly take them in.

"What?"

"They want you back in Australia. Your government requests that we turn straight back to Darwin. It's not, of course, on our route. Our route's Sydney-Hong Kong, no stops."

All Duquesne's drowsiness fled. He was speechless with horror.

Standing there facing the pilot he felt his blood racing again and mouthed: "What's it all about?"

"You're a scientist, aren't you, Dr. Duquesne?" asked the New Zealander. "For security reasons you are not permitted to travel outside of Australia. It's all I've been told."

"You'll put me down? You'll go back to Darwin? Because the crackpots . . ."

"I've refused." The pilot was grim-faced. "I don't consider it a legitimate request on the part of the Australian government. When the request was received we were already beyond Darwin. The thing's absurd. But I decided to tell you in case there's anything you want to do."

"Is that all they told you? It was for security reasons?" demanded Duquesne.

The captain stared back at him.

"You're travelling with a girl, Irina Grigorieva. The Australian authorities have informed me she is known to be under the control of the Russians and that you are to be told this."

"What!" Duquesne shouted, above the roar of the engines. "You're crazy! They're crazy! It's bullshit."

But fear gripped him, and instinctively he felt that what the pilot had been told was the truth.

"You should never have got through the passport check," added the New Zealander. "It was never intended."

"Then, how did I, for Christ's sake?"

"There was a slip-up somewhere." The New Zealander's face relaxed slightly, crinkling round the eyes. "Office tie-ups—too much red tape. They get enmeshed." His lips smiled slightly with the professional's contempt for the bureaucrats.

"You'll hand me over in Hong Kong?" asked Duquesne dully.

"I'll do nothing," said the other, eyeing Duquesne. "I'm the captain of this ship, that's all. They want you, they'll arrange a reception committee when you get in. That's all." He set his lips, and said casually: "I thought I'd warn you."

Duquesne swung heavily out of the cabin and after a moment went into the washroom. It was the first-class one, up front, and there was a little seat, on which he collapsed, staring at his strained face in the mirror. While the captain had talked, his mind had been on Irina, fitting pieces together with such ease, working so coolly that the emotions sweeping him seemed part of someone else.

She was under the control of the Russians, was she? What did he himself really know of her? As methodically as he could, he went back over their relationship. He thought of Vasily Sanin and the several times he had seen them together. Then he chanced to remember that little camera which Irina had been carrying. And how later he had found that his scientific papers on the wheat had been disturbed.

This must mean that the Russians wanted his wheat, too. Irina, with her slow and mocking smile, the sideways glance, the slim and velvety body made for love. Irina, with her gallantry and readiness to gamble and her love of risks. Irina the fake. The double-dealer.

Duquesne sat fighting, gazing unseeingly in the mirror, fighting grief, fighting his wounded pride and outrage. His head dropped to his hands and he sat there shaking. "Oh Christ," he whispered. "Christ help me."

In the little cramped cubicle he stayed grappling with his sudden loneliness and isolation, his imminent betrayal. Finally a peremptory knocking forced him to open the door. The Asian steward said enquiringly, "You all right, sir?" with a relieved expression as Duquesne walked out.

He went back, down the middle of the pulsating cabin. Irina still dozed. He took a vacant seat across the aisle from her and began thinking as coolly as he could.

The Americans wanted him dead. On two counts, if they had discovered how Dick Temple had died. They would want to avenge Dick's death, and they wanted him out of the way because of the wheat. That much was proved. And he was meant to be virtually a prisoner in Australia. Now the Russians wanted him—but presumably on a different basis. They must want him *for* his wheat. They had serious production problems, that was well known. But the political implications could be even more important—the Soviet gift to the world's hungry. And, Duquesne started—as Blantyre himself had pointed out—a vindication of Lysenko. The Russian motives were clear. Duquesne would make a first-class prize.

Surely his only hope was to publicise his discovery as soon as possible? Where? How? His eyes went to his briefcase, where in a concealed pocket was a complete technical report. He had posted to himself in London a sample of seeds, and Jerry held more in Australia. Why not publicise it? Why not at the United Nations conference? But he would not get there now. He would be a virtual prisoner of the Australians the moment he set foot in Hong Kong. Unless he escaped. Unless he was cleverer than any of them.

As Irina stirred and he saw her eyelashes flutter, he dropped his head forward on his chest and closed his eyes. He needed more time.

Irina obviously did not yet know the Australians had spotted her. How long had they been watching her—watching them both? Lying there with his eyes shut, Duquesne trembled with anger. Easy to see Irina in her new role now, looking back. How cleverly she had played her part. The riding school, Vasily Sanin with his insistent questions. Irina, who was a fake. And yet—his heart ached—how he loved her, had loved her. He sat there, fighting off an impulse to get up, take hold of her, hurt her. Blood beat in his throat, and his hands clenched on the arm rests.

The only card he held was to keep quiet what he knew. If he let Irina go on thinking he was ignorant of her role, he might be in a stronger position. Should he tell her of the efforts to have him landed at Darwin?

He had never told Irina anything of his work, of the wheat. Should he tell her now the necessary minimum at least? He would say nothing, he decided, only act normally—as normally as he could.

# CHAPTER THREE

Engines whining and singing, the plane hung poised in the sunset, over the dark volcanic hills which rose up steeply from the waters of the harbour. Irina's fingers clutched Duquesne's, and they gave themselves to the drama of landing on a runway a mile out on the water, watching the sculptured motionless Chinese waves, the white plastic skyscrapers massed around the shore and balancing among the dense green hills. The sun dropped below the horizon, and in a blaze of artificial lights the airplane thudded gently down.

Twenty minutes later, in the brightness of the immigration-hall, Duquesne stood gripping Irina's elbow. He was swept with successive waves of sadness and despair for his love of her and her betrayal.

At the checkpoint their passports were inspected by a round-faced Chinese clerk. Once through the barrier, Irina gave a little sigh and began to speak, but the words died on her lips as they were accosted from behind. Turning, Duquesne surveyed the bespectacled young man in a tropical suit. He looked for others and then thought: So as yet there's only one of them. For the man was alone.

"You're certainly Dr. Duquesne! Simpson's my name. . . ."

The practised tones and easy informality of the young Australian diplomat.

Duquesne drawled: "A social occasion, is it? Has your handbook a section on this kind of thing?"

The man laughed and made as though to clap him on the back, but then stopped abruptly. Beside him, Duquesne felt Irina's tautness as she looked on watchfully.

Duquesne said flatly, "It's been nice meeting you. We have to get our bags now," and began strolling away, steering a course for himself and Irina through the big hall. Irina ran to keep up with him, and they knew Simpson followed.

Waiting at the luggage-chute, Duquesne kept up his studied rejection of any relationship between himself and Simpson, who stayed close behind. He was uncertain of the other's powers. At least Simpson was alone. The Australians were playing it casually so far, but there would probably be more of them outside.

When their bags finally came, porters vied excitedly to take them, with victory to the toughest and biggest. But Simpson had been quick, and was talking suddenly in rapid Chinese, and the porter nodded, changed direction and made off quickly with his trolley to a side-door. They ran after him, down corridors, outside into the hot moist darkness, and found themselves in a compound with parked cars, a taxi rank, a dense crowd of Chinese. Simpson's voice said at Duquesne's ear: "We've a car for you. This way, please." Duquesne swung round and sighted a waiting limousine. The doors were open, and two Europeans were getting out.

Without warning, Duquesne was pushed from behind. A furious altercation was occurring among the crowd, and he felt a surge of bodies against them. He saw Simpson's face, his mouth open in protest, but in a moment Simpson had disappeared behind a mass of flailing bodies, working men in singlets and pants, swaying back and forth, shouting. Somehow a wedge had been driven between them and Simpson, but the porter was still with them. Desperately Duquesne grabbed at him.

Borne inexorably along among the yelling Chinese, Duquesne soon saw it was a mock fight, of pushing, jostling, glancing blows, that he was himself shouting, but more often than not the Chinese round him were laughing.

Simpson and the limousine had disappeared. Then all at once the crowd around them thinned and fell away, and he saw they had covered ground in the confusion and were at the other side of the parking lot. The trolley man, miraculously still with them, indicated a waiting taxi. Shaken and panting, they fell into it. The driver hastily banged down the boot-lid on their bags and, throwing himself at the wheel, made rapidly off.

"Who is Simpson?" Irina's voice was shaking.

"You didn't recognise the Foreign Affairs mould?"

"What did he want?"

"Me, my dear. Surely you realised that was a reception committee?" Duquesne raised his voice and addressed the driver. "Go to the Star Ferry. We want to cross to Hong Kong Island."

The man said over his shoulder: "You go town."

"No, Star Ferry."

"Not Tlar Ferry."

"*Yes,* Star Ferry! What the bloody hell!" Duquesne began to lose his temper. He was still breathing hard from the rough handling at the airport.

"Town for Lantao," said the man.

"He's saying 'tunnel,' not 'town.' It would be quicker for Lantao, of course," said Irina suddenly.

"Ah, yes, I suppose so. Under the harbour."

"Better tunnel for Lantao." The man's round shoulders were bent absorbedly over his wheel. His head was grey and close-shaven, with a motheaten look.

"All right. Then to the ferry pier at Connaught Road Central."

Irina twisted her head to look at Duquesne.

"Simpson would have stopped you?"

"Obviously, if that very useful diversion had not taken place."

"Why, Jack?"

"Just a little bit of hush-hush work I've been doing. They thought I needed an—escort, I suppose."

"They don't want you to go to Rome?"

Duquesne exclaimed suddenly, "How the hell . . ." and stopped. He thought to himself: How did the driver know we were going to Lantao? No one told him.

Lantao had been Irina's idea. She had heard of the *pension* from friends.

Irina's voice trembled as she breathed: "Jack, will they stop you leaving Hong Kong?"

"Of course, that remains to be seen. Hong Kong is a big city, and you've arranged such a nice hideaway, haven't you, my dear, at Lantao?"

Even to himself his tone was false, his words bogus. "My dear," he was saying, with its connotations of marital boredom.

They were driving as though the devil were after them. On the wide boulevard the sickly arc lights regularly flashed on Irina's face, and Duquesne suddenly shivered in the air-conditioning of the taxi.

As they entered the harbour tunnel, Irina said, trying to recapture their old trust and intimacy: "Not as romantic an introduction to Hong Kong as we wanted, Jack. Thank goodness for the ferry. It will be an hour's ride on it."

Her hand felt for his. But Duquesne had hauled out his pocket book and was thumbing through it in the white brilliance of the tunnel lights, and didn't notice the hand.

Later, on the Lantao ferry-boat, they sat outside on the top deck, the summer night streaming away on either side, and listened to the *slish slish* of the water. The lights of Hong Kong quivered and gleamed up and down its heights.

Irina turned her slanting eyes from the grandeur of the harbour and leaned back over the railing, sliding a hand along to close on Duquesne's, beseeching a response from him; but his face when he turned to her was cold, and he said, at his most matter-of-fact and Australian: "There's a bar inside. Feel like a beer?"

Putting in to the pier in Silvermine Bay, Lantao hung a rugged dark mass above them, strings of lights resolved into a huddle of stalls and shops and rough eating places. Fishing vessels, junks and sampans trembled gently at their anchors.

They waited until the crowd thinned and then went ashore. Duquesne, keeping an eye on the porter who had their bags, walked slightly behind Irina. He half-saw a solitary European figure, broad against the slightly built Asians, move over towards the shadow of a group of stalls. It was impossible. Vasily Sanin belonged in Canberra. He could not be here in Lantao. He began to say "Look!" to Irina and then abruptly changed it to "I'll be back in a moment," nodding towards the Gentlemen sign down the road. He dumped their hand luggage down and, retaining only his briefcase, hurried off. Beyond the sign, he turned the corner, out of sight.

He stopped, counted twelve slowly and deliberately, and then turned back. Irina and the European had come together. Duquesne saw the man nod and walk rapidly away. Duquesne had moved out of sight of Irina before she had turned to walk the few steps back to the porter and their bags.

He joined her, and they walked slowly and without speaking to the main road. The two waiting buses were already filled. Duquesne and Irina paused irresolutely and were immediately addressed by a young man in a dark suit with a vaguely hall-porterish cap.

"You are here for the Golden Dragon Hotel, sir and lady?"

"Yes."

"Please. Your bags. Here is car." And he motioned them in.

"Short distance only," the dark suit added, as the car smoothed its way along the pitted surface past stalls lit by bare bulbs, filled with the cheap and the colourful.

The wide bay circled out of sight as the car turned up the steep hill. Its headlamps picked out a police Land-rover turning off just ahead of them to a side-road. Duquesne felt unexpectedly glad to see it.

Moments later they, too, turned off the road and into the courtyard of a substantial building. "Hotel Golden Dragon," the illuminated sign insisted.

"I think we will like it," said Irina. Her voice was both appealing and determined.

Duquesne wondered how she had managed to get a black smut just slightly below the left cheekbone. How it suited her, this chance beauty-spot.

The hotel was reassuringly normal. An adequate entrance. Cane furniture in the modest square foyer, and a boy who took their bags at once. There was nobody at the desk.

"Shouldn't we register?" asked Duquesne, but the boy gestured to them to follow. They went up one flight of stairs, turned left, passing a smiling Chinese lady seated at a side-table sewing, and entered their room two doors further on. Irina at once drew the curtains aside and pulled Duquesne to the window, revealing a hemisphere of countless small lights, pinpricks in the velvet of the darkened sea and the sombre gauze of the night sky.

Duquesne said what he felt was expected of him and then turned to Irina.

"You're so tired. Have your bath now and we'll go to bed. We don't want more to eat now."

Irina smiled. She loved prolonged hot baths, the sandalwood essence she used giving the water a fragrance which had seemed so foreign in Australia.

"And you'll come and dry me later," she commanded.

Duquesne waited until she was in the scented water. Then he took his big briefcase, which contained his toilet gear, a change of clothes, a copy of *The Voyage of the Beagle* he was rereading, and his technical papers on the wheat. He removed Irina's passport and ticket, which he had been carrying. Then he checked the combination lock of his bag and went out. Without looking back, he closed the door of the room quietly, walked casually past the smiling Chinese lady and down the stairs. The lobby was still empty.

Outside, he merged immediately with the darkness. His rubber-soled shoes silent on the concrete path, he went straight out of the gates and walked rapidly back down the road. Only ten minutes had gone by since Irina began her bath. Where was Sanin? With the feeling that eyes watched from the darkness, Duquesne hurried on, a man alone now.

The last ferry for Hong Kong left at 10.15, according to his tourist pamphlet. It was now ten o'clock. Driving himself now, his body stale and rancid from the long hours of travel and the developments of the last couple of hours, he nevertheless made good time.

Down near the pier the open-air stalls still drew their customers. People were sitting out at wooden benches in a restaurant under coloured lights. Smells of fish and the sea were strong, and Duquesne thought he could distinguish the odour of the mashed shrimp which they made into shrimp paste somewhere—he had read—around here.

It was only five minutes past ten when he walked hurriedly into the terminal building once more, only to pull up with a start. The ticket office was shut. A Chinese with an enormous broom was sweeping the floor. Duquesne advanced on a man who looked vaguely official and said: "Ferry—Hong Kong!"

But the man, shrugging, pointed to the closed window of the ticket office, showed his teeth and led Duquesne to a noticeboard.

"Felly go at ten. . . ."

Beaming, he waved a hand, and Duquesne saw, now far from shore, the three decks of lights of the last steamer. He stood and swore, a scattering of people gathering to watch his discomfiture.

"No more ferries tonight?"

"No felly. Tomorrow felly. . . ."

Duquesne's heart sank, and he strode down the pier. Standing morosely by the swaying fishing boats, he felt a hand pluck his sleeve.

"Kai-do, kai-do." An old man with a lined face spoke volubly and almost incomprehensibly to Duquesne. It seemed the man would take him in a vessel anchored near.

"This one?" barked Duquesne, pointing. It was a junk, a very modest junk. "Motor?"

"Motor!" Oh, of course a motor. The man had a good motor, a new motor.

"How long?"

"One hour and a half to Hong Kong."

"How much?"

The man held up both hands, with all fingers outstretched.

"One thousand Hong Kong dollars!"

Duquesne laughed, and turned away.

"Nine hundred," the man called, chasing after him.

Duquesne considered. It was a lot. But he could not afford to wait on Lantao. He nodded agreement.

Boarding the junk, he urged the man to hurry. He was not to be the only occupant. Immediately about half a dozen others climbed on board, too.

"Who are these?"

"Flend and my family. . . ."

The man probably ran the junk regularly to the mainland and back. But the motor started up with a healthy roar, and the breeze ripped past as they manoeuvred out into the darkness, putting a merciful distance between Duquesne and the Golden Dragon Hotel—and Sanin. And Irina.

"You go Kowloon now. Tsim sha tsui. OK?"

It would be better for him in Kowloon. They might be looking for him in the Connaught Road pier. They would think he had made the last ferry back, probably.

"I want a hotel," said Duquesne to the man. "No passport, no papers."

The news was received with a broad smile.

"You pay money. Good hotel. Girl come to room."

Duquesne let the suggestion remain.

The taxi edged as close to the kerb as possible before stopping, avoiding the pushing Chinese, the camera-covered European tourists, darting boys carrying the world's merchandise. Quick-eyed Chinese shopkeepers still stood at their doors.

"Wait," said the man who had accompanied Duquesne from the *kai-do.* He disappeared into a doorway and quickly re-emerged. "No name needed. Two hun'd dollar for me. Girls come."

Duquesne was glad to pay and hoped girls wouldn't come. Inside, the impassive Chinese at the desk simply gave him a key and told Duquesne to telephone for what he wanted.

The room was plain, rectangular, the plaster just beginning to peel. The water pressure was low but enough for him to brush his teeth and to have some sort of shower. He fastened the bolt, turned down the noisy air-conditioning unit and fell into a deep sleep.

# CHAPTER FOUR

His watch said 5 a.m. when he awoke from a long dream of fire, which had swept the street below, having begun in a faulty lead to one of the perpendicular advertisement signs that ran up and down buildings all along the streets. Sirens were actually sounding, but their sound soon faded. Sunlight—not flames—was outside, sunlight not to be denied. As he licked dry lips, his troubles assailed him in a massive onslaught, but his brain, refreshed, assembled facts coolly.

To return to Australia was to return to what had become a prison. To a straitjacket of inactivity. They would never develop his wheat and they would never trust him now because of Irina. The Americans seemed even more anxious to muzzle him. They had tried to kill him. And now the Russians came into the picture in some way which he did not yet fully understand. The Russians, fully briefed by Irina.

His one hope was the Rome meeting, where he would be able to give his discovery to the world by means of the United Nations. But until he got to the conference he was in grave danger. Would he make it out of Hong Kong? Would the Australians have an extradition agreement with the Hong Kong government? It was likely. Which meant that, even if he had thrown off the Embassy people, the moment his passport signalled his presence at the airport he would be taken into custody.

With sudden decision he shot out of bed and reached for the telephone. Five-twenty a.m., which would make it after 7 a.m. in Australia. He thumbed through his notebook.

"I want to call Australia. A personal call to Mr. John Silkin at this number in Sydney."

He had to wait, and sat in his singlet and pants on the side of the bed, concentrating. Searching for Silkin's number, he had come across the name of one Bill Crane, Silkin's friend, and Silkin's words came back to him.

"If I don't hear from you or you can't get through, I'll rely on you to leave a message with Bill."

Bill Crane worked at Hong Kong television. Quite suddenly, Duquesne had a plan so simple and daring that he brought his palm down on the bed with tremendous force and, getting up, paced excitedly.

When the phone rang, Silkin's voice came through so clearly he might have been in the room next door.

"I'd expected a quiet holiday, but even in Hong Kong I'm much in demand," said Duquesne grimly. He tried to veil his meaning. "My compatriots wanted me to return quick smart to Sydney. Then they had a reception committee ready for me on arrival, but new actors in the game—new to me anyway—got me away. They apparently want to beg, borrow or steal my product." He paused and then went on, his voice flat and unemotional: "Then I found my travelling companion had arranged another and quite different reception committee. This was a complete surprise to me. But I *think* I've evaded them both. Now. Can you tell me, has our mutual friend in Canberra—ah—surfaced?"

Silkin gave himself time to catch up a little.

"You timed your call well," he said. "One or two enquiries had been directed to the lady next door, and she got worried and reported his absence. But he hasn't turned up yet, so not to worry. I don't quite understand all these reception committees."

"I'm going to get in touch with your friend here," said Duquesne. "Not socially, though. I thought I could give him some copy. A fillip for his news sessions. Just a preliminary to what could come later. You'll be hearing from me."

Duquesne rang off, feeling much better. He went into the bathroom, and shaved and showered in the limited water. Then he called for tea and toast.

It was nearly seven. He consulted his notebook and dialled Bill Crane's number. By a stroke of luck Crane came on the line at once, bracing and welcoming.

"I'm afraid it's early," Duquesne said apologetically.

"Not for these parts. I'm up at six regularly. Beating the heat, you see. I'm delighted to hear from you." He spoke with the confident accents of the Australian upper classes. His breezy tones were a tonic. He invited Duquesne to meet him that afternoon at three o'clock in the Mandarin Bar in Queen's Road Central.

Duquesne went out and, closing his mind to trouble, spent some hours killing time, mingling with the crowd in Cameron Road—a little cheap, a little closed in—and then in elegant Nathan Road. He looked at jade and at elaborate ivory temples and fat Buddhas. He bought a fawn safari-suit and other clothes.

He got to the Mandarin Bar early. Crane was handsome, inclined to stoutness, with the arrogant head of a Roman emperor. But he was easy to talk to and had a quick understanding.

"You're Australia's most highly regarded plant scientist, Dr. Duquesne," he said. "Anything you care to say will make an impact. And you want to make an announcement over our TV? What is it? Or what is it about?"

Duquesne answered slowly: "I'm afraid I am not prepared to tell you that in advance. But I will guarantee it will create a sensation. Nothing less."

"Are you completely serious about this, Dr. Duquesne?"

"I could not be more so."

Crane looked hard at him. Could the bloody fool really have something, or was he off his head? Certainly his reputation was deserved. Crane had done his homework. But his editor was tough and cynical. And nearly always right. Crane came to a sudden decision.

"We'll tape an interview around this time tomorrow. You prepare the questions that I will use. My editor, and only my editor, will hear the tape. If he says yes, then you go on the air on the nine o'clock news. That's the top hour. Excerpts from your interview will first be given and then I'll interview you. This will be broadcast live. Agreed?"

"Right," said Duquesne.

Crane felt reassured. If Duquesne were in the least phoney, he would be asking for money in advance. They all did.

"Money," said Duquesne. "I must change some of my money. Where is the nearest place?"

Duquesne idled his way back to his hotel. He did not know quite what to do. He went into a Chinese cinema. The shouts, the brassy music, the firecrackers were too much. Finally, it was 6 p.m. and he was back at his hotel.

Upstairs, he called for a bottle of Scotch and ice. It came quickly, and he poured a substantial drink. Could things be worse? Yes, they could be worse. He was not yet a pawn on a chessboard and he wouldn't be. Unbidden, Irina's treachery intruded, and he groaned with the sharpness of the memory. Sitting on the edge of the bed, he sipped his whisky and suffered. He knew that the present scene would be repeated many times.

There was a quiet knock on the door. Surprised, he got up to open it. Outside in the passage stood a tall merry-faced man. A European.

# CHAPTER FIVE

Duquesne was too confounded to react quickly.

"Who are you?" he demanded.

Even as he spoke, the pride he had felt in his escape, in his swift decision to act, went in an instant. Warily, he took the card the other held out and read:

Dmitry Dmitrich Menshikov,
Learned Secretary, Praesidium of Academy of Plant Sciences

"Dr. Duquesne, I am hopeful that you might know of me. I know *your* work well."

Menshikov. Duquesne stood back and awkwardly motioned the other into the shabby room, gesturing vaguely towards the untidy bed, the one hard chair, the bottle. The Russian watched Duquesne's face comprehend the situation. Then he plumped down on the chair. He was sweating.

"The air-conditioning doesn't work too well," said Duquesne, playing it slowly.

Menshikov accepted a drink and tossed half of it down in a way that reminded Duquesne of Irina. Fortunately, there were two glasses.

"I hadn't expected anyone. Certainly not someone like you," said Duquesne.

"Naturally. I'm not officially here. I'm really at a meeting in New York. I'm here on your account. Yours only." His English was almost perfect. "I want to talk. Come out to dinner, where it is cooler. At my hotel they told me everyone should go to one of the revolving restaurants and look at the lights. They said the food was good, too."

Duquesne regarded the handsome face for a moment. Menshikov must be in his fifties. His work had become known in the West only in the last few years and had quickly given him a world reputation, but it had been the culmination of some twenty years of sustained and brilliant developments which had gone unremarked at the time, even in his own country. Starting in the late part of the Khrushchev era, Menshikov had become a regular attender at scientific meetings in the United States and Europe. Duquesne was impressed and puzzled. Shrugging slightly, he nodded his acceptance.

They walked out of the hotel and found a taxi where Cameron Road joined Chatham Road to sweep around the harbour. As they drove, Menshikov talked of the meeting he had just attended on plant tissue culture. Professionalism immediately dominated, Hong Kong fell away, and they might have been in a laboratory. Duquesne looked with interest at his companion, taking in his elegance and sensing an underlying toughness, while their common enthusiasms demolished nationality.

As they left the taxi, Hong Kong once more embraced them with its movement, its glitter and its cheerfulness. They entered a slightly shabby lift in a building in Nathan Road and were shot twenty storeys to the Juno Restaurant. There was no difficulty about a table, and they were fortunate enough to get one in the outer ring, next to the windows.

Menshikov's fine eyes glittered in the candlelight as he looked across the table at Duquesne and said: "I have stage-managed it all so well, don't you agree?"

Frail scattered jewels gleamed and winked against black velvet, as Hong Kong slid slowly by. Chinese boys darted with steaming plates. They waited for their Peking duck to be cooked and drank more whisky.

"I will be very simple, Dr. Duquesne," said Menshikov. "We know much about you. Don't be offended, I do beg you. We consider you one of the top men in your field. You already had a good reputation, and what we think you have now accomplished with your wheat would be confirmation. Our information is that you are responsible for the identification of a new strain with unique adaptation to growing conditions which were previously thought completely inhospitable to wheat." He laughed. "Your authorities thought it so important that they put the plants under what was virtually military guard—and then apparently burned them rather than chance them falling into the hands of the Americans! But you will have seeds somewhere."

Duquesne was rigid with concentration. The great hill on the other side of the harbour tiptoed past his unseeing eyes. It must have been Irina somehow. And others. Did they know of the death of Dick Temple and of his underwater entombment? No, that would be impossible. He forced rationality to his thoughts.

"I am authorised to offer you a position as director of your own wheat institute in the Ukraine. This would be a largely autonomous division within the institute of which I am in charge. We can discuss details later, but I can assure you now that you would have complete freedom to develop the wheat further. You would be expected to ensure that developing countries all around the world are encouraged to use it—as, indeed, they should want to—and you would have large funds at your disposal to do so. The work would entail frequent travelling throughout the world."

Menshikov paused, regarding Duquesne thoughtfully.

"When people from the West come to work and live in the Soviet Union," he continued, "it is always said that they have defected. Some have, but there would be no hint of it in your case. It would be more like the British scientists who went to help Fidel Castro get his agriculture going. Or like the Italians who are selling us their expertise in automobile manufacture. You would simply be coming to us on a lucrative contract for whatever period you wanted. And a damn lucrative contract. We suggest four hundred thousand U.S. dollars a year. No tax, of course. Most would be paid—if you wished—into a Swiss bank account. You could live—what is the English expression, 'like a lord'?—on the rest and still probably save."

Two waiters arrived with their Peking duck. Menshikov's face wreathed in smiles and he tucked his napkin in his shirtfront as they began wrapping pieces of duck and spring onion in the thin pancakes, dousing them in soy sauce, while the waiter filled the delicate teacups.

Duquesne said: "Your interest in the Soviet Union is in winter wheat, not in my variety. Development of my wheat must take place in the tropics, so it would be of no use to the U.S.S.R."

"Russia also has the interests of underdeveloped countries at heart.

We are not acting stupidly in making our offer to you. Russia also suffers from the problem of drought. *And* we plan to spend massively on cereal research in the U.S.S.R. More than the United States."

Duquesne said: "But what about theories of genetics that are still the basis of so much of your plant breeding—I speak of 'directed training,' of course. Lysenko's theories."

"They are not the basis of my plant breeding," said Menshikov with conviction. "Nor yours, despite the apparent support your discovery gives to Lysenko's ideas. If some scientists still remain who carved out careers for themselves on the basis of his theories, and who escaped—er—reproach later on, when Stalin died . . ."

"Escaped being put to death, you mean?"

Menshikov grinned.

"Well, if you like. They certainly survived, Doctor."

"Vavilov didn't survive," said Duquesne quietly. "One of the most eminent and widely respected scientists in the game."

Menshikov did not respond.

"I want to live," said Duquesne, in a matter-of-fact way.

"And you've managed to, Doctor, up till now," said Menshikov, eyeing Duquesne. "But perhaps not entirely without luck?"

Duquesne started.

"And Australia—it has promoted your discovery, Doctor? Or perhaps the United States would have treated you better?"

Duquesne said cautiously: "A small country, mine, you know, without much experience at the international level. . . ."

"Please don't talk what our American colleagues call crap," said Menshikov unexpectedly, but with a smile. "All countries can act occasionally in ways which embarrass their citizens. Mine more than most. But yours, too. To say nothing of the United States."

After a pause, he continued.

"Doctor, the offer of a post can only be welcome if it provides something better than your present job. Perhaps I err. My informants may have read the picture wrongly. If, indeed, you are content in Australia, why, this offer is naturally obnoxious and we'll simply enjoy our duck. Not bad, this duck, eh? Not greasy, as they warn one. Afterwards we will take the soup, you agree?"

"Lysenko would represent a problem," said Duquesne, disregarding him. "In view of my own work recently."

"Because your wheat would be claimed to have become drought resistant by being forced to assimilate tropical conditions and acquiring new characteristics?"

Duquesne shrugged. "At the Mironovka Institute . . ." he began.

"Dr. Duquesne!" broke in Menshikov. "At my own institute we have always followed classical theory, with excellent results." He put down his piece of duck and wiped his mouth. "I am a man of science first, and then a Russian. As a man of science—you know it also, for you know my work—I bow to no theory, no political system. And this has been possible despite Lysenko. He simply lost me time. Can I take it that your career has been thus trouble-free?"

Looking at his angry face, Duquesne began to like him.

More quietly, Menshikov then said: "Doctor, I speak the truth when I repeat that your actual work would be completely free of political interference and when I say that as a member of my group of institutes you would have much intercourse with the developing countries and with the West. We would not otherwise be offering you work, since your particular wheat is connected with the tropics."

Menshikov finished his soup in silence and then called for cognac.

"What will you do, Doctor, if you do not come to me?" he asked.

"I must consider it," said Duquesne, his sombre eyes sliding away from the Russian's, ignoring the question. "If I came to the Soviet Union on the sort of arrangement you are talking about, there is no one I would sooner throw my lot in with than you. I need time to think it over." He added, testing him: "I'm off to Rome next week. There is a grains meeting beginning there the second day of June."

Menshikov's hand came down with a clap on the table.

"You give me hope! We'll drink to it!"

They raised and clinked glasses.

"I have two days here, Doctor," Menshikov continued. "I leave not tomorrow, but the following morning. I am here for questions at the Peninsula Hotel, at this telephone number."

They lingered over their drinks, drawn by the fragile beauty outside the enormous ceiling-to-floor windows. Walking out, Menshikov threw a convivial arm around Duquesne's shoulders.

"We'll meet at six tomorrow, shall we? Not here again. . . ." He laughed with pleasure. "One doesn't wish to pay a second visit and lose any of the flavour of Hong Kong at night. And, Doctor, I hope—please believe me—that for your own sake you may accept our offer."

And they went down and out into the warm night. Duquesne thought to himself that now he knew at least one of the ways in which an approach was made from the other political world. It was very civilised. And clever. And dependable?

# CHAPTER SIX

BACK IN HIS HOTEL ROOM, Duquesne poured himself a last drink and tried to think of Crane's questions—fruitlessly for a time because part of him was back in the restaurant with Menshikov. Then, resolutely, he forced his brain to order to compose his own television interview.

He tossed and sweated on his bed until five in the morning, reliving the highly coloured evening, his brain still racing from the cognac, straining to encompass Menshikov's startling proposition, the reality of which escaped him every so often, in the haunting Hong Kong night.

"Christ, though, I'd be tempted—if I hadn't seen Crane first." And from the safety of his previous decision he reassessed the dangerous charm of Menshikov and the substance of his offer.

At five he searched through his gear and found a sleeping pill, his last thought being that Menshikov, who did not leave till the morning after it, would certainly see or hear of that nine o'clock broadcast.

At noon Crane phoned.

"Could you meet me for lunch—let me see . . ."

"Why not the same place?"

"No." A pause. "Meet me at the Blue Sky Restaurant, number forty-six Nanking Street, beyond Jordan Road."

"I'll bring my prepared stuff with me," Duquesne promised.

"Yes. One o'clock, then."

Over lunch, Crane looked nervy and excited, his eyes curious as they rested on Duquesne.

"It can't be done," he announced.

"It can't?"

"My editor won't go for it. He's a timorous fellow and he had a rap over the knuckles recently about his handling of the Philippine elections. He doesn't want to risk getting another government against him, particularly as he comes from Melbourne himself and knows how bloody rough Australian authorities can be."

"On what grounds?" asked Duquesne. Crane's news was a knockout, but this mustn't be shown.

Crane caught the waitress's eye, and they were served beer. Other girls brought spring rolls and pork dumplings.

"My boss always plays extra-safe. He checked with Australia. He rang—"

"CSIRO?"

Crane's eyes were everywhere. Perhaps he was merely seeking soy sauce.

"Yes. He spoke to Sir John Doughty."

"I see. And?"

Crane shrugged.

"Doughty said surely there must be some mistake. He said"—Crane fished in his pocket, pulling out a crumpled paper—"he said, in full: 'Dr. Duquesne has no authority whatsoever to make any statement over your television on work in progress in CSIRO. He is a staff member of this organisation and as such he is obliged to observe the normal rules regarding the release of information. Should he not observe these rules, which are a standard condition of employment in CSIRO, the Australian government would have no hesitation in holding you responsible for knowingly abetting Dr. Duquesne in his unethical behaviour and would immediately make the strongest representations to the Hong Kong authorities. And at the highest level.' "

"Yes," admitted Duquesne. "That's quite impressive. Apparently enough to make your boss wet his pants."

"Well, he hopes to keep his job. Shortly after that the embassy was on to him. Then they were on to me. 'Classified material' was the 'in' phrase."

Duquesne was suddenly furious. Crane poured more beer. They drank, and Crane asked: "What are your plans?"

Speaking with care, just controlling his flood of feeling, Duquesne replied: "Ah, that's the question. My plans. My plans might have to be changed now."

Crane, his eyes intent on him, said: "My boss tells me the Embassy are very keen to . . . catch up with you."

"Uh-huh. Expecting one of them here, are you?"

Crane snapped: "I chose this place, on the contrary, rather carefully. Not a soul knows we're here."

"Thanks," Duquesne muttered. "I suppose I needn't expect anyone to be waiting back at the hotel, either."

"If they are, I didn't send them. Hell damn it, the Embassy are combing the bloody place, and my boss is pals with the first secretary. I happen to have disclaimed all knowledge of your hotel or any details at all about you."

Duquesne said flatly: "That's good of you."

Crane continued: "They tried all they knew on my boss. They told him a court injunction is under way to enable them to apply to the Hong Kong government for your extradition."

"Oh Christ," said Duquesne in a tired way, slumping back in his chair, while his brain raced. "A leper could hardly be less welcome company. Thanks for the warning." He got up to go. "I appreciate your . . . reticence."

"Oh, sit down," said Crane. "White men don't come to this place." He grinned, and beckoned the waitress. "We'll drink to your successful extrication from this mess. And I never did like red tape."

Outside in the full glare of early afternoon, his fear now outweighed humiliation. He wondered if he was wanted also in connection with Dick Temple's death. They would stop him leaving Hong Kong, and thus forbid him attendance at the United Nations meeting in Rome. Or else they would induce the Hong Kong authorities to put him on a plane for Australia. The old scenario was now erased. A new one must be written. And he had the means at hand.

Menshikov's offer last night had been intoxicating but forbidden; it had formed an exotic interlude. This afternoon, in the light of Crane's disclosure, it reconstituted itself as a solid alternative. For two hours Duquesne walked, and when he got back to the hotel his mind was made up. He bathed, changed, drank a beer and went to the Peninsula Hotel to meet Menshikov.

Menshikov, impressive in a cream tropical suit, was more handsome than ever against the colonial splendour of the public rooms. He threw an arm briefly round Duquesne's shoulders in the remembered gesture and led him to a private room. A waiter brought vodka and a bottle of Ballantine's Twelve Years Old.

"Your favourite," said Menshikov, waving a hand at the whisky.

Duquesne looked at the long-fingered well-shaped hand and at the direct good-humoured face, and felt his robust approval of the previous night once more take hold of him. As the whisky slid down his throat insidious well-being crept over him, soothing away the memory of the raw and sweat-soaked hours in the alien streets outside, giving him back a measure of his self-respect.

Menshikov was exultant at Duquesne's acceptance, bouncing up from his chair to wring his hands.

"You'll not regret it, Doctor," he declared seriously. "As one scientist to another I can assure you of that. I wish you to consider it a not irrevocable step, one that will leave you a free man in the years to come, free to research the depths of your subject without restraints or interference. Otherwise I would not make you this offer."

He talked at length, sketching in initial programmes of work, explaining the terms of the contract, describing the Ukraine.

"The official offer you will receive in Rome. In the meantime, there are practical details to be attended to. You must get out of Hong Kong, and we have taken the liberty of arranging your travel to Rome."

Menshikov rang the bell and told the waiter to call Mr. Bogdanov. Mr. Bogdanov was short and compact with an impassive watchful face. Menshikov said he would leave them together. He had to leave Hong Kong that night after all, as he was now en route to see a colleague in Prague. He wrung Duquesne's hand until it hurt as he said goodbye and hurried from the room.

Mr. Bogdanov said: "It is best you leave Hong Kong quickly. We have made bookings by an indirect route. London, via Singapore. You go not to Rome, then, but to Pisa, where you go by road to Rome. It is all set out on this sheet."

Duquesne looked at his itinerary and said: "Of course, the big stumbling block is getting out of Hong Kong. And I want to stop off in London for at least a day."

"Leaving Hong Kong is taken care of," said Mr. Bogdanov quickly. "It will not be expected that you go back in the direction of Australia. You leave Hong Kong for Singapore, that is. We take photographs now, and tomorrow morning a new passport will be ready—just for the journey. Then you continue with your own passport after you arrive in Italy."

He telephoned, and another man entered with a camera and flash-light. In silence the photographs were taken.

"You leave tomorrow evening," said Mr. Bogdanov. "Your tickets will be delivered to your hotel tomorrow with the passport, all in the name of James Gleason, an Australian from Melbourne. You will be issued with sufficient sterling for London and enough lire to enable you to hire a car in Pisa and drive it down to this address in Rome. There you will receive money for your needs until after the conference is over. You cannot without danger change your own traveller's cheques here or in London or Rome. I think"—for a moment Bogdanov's eyes searched the far distance before returning to rest on Duquesne—"I think that all is in order."

Somehow Duquesne had not the slightest doubt that it was all in order or that it would go very smoothly to plan.

Mr. Bogdanov hesitated as he took his leave.

"There is no one you wish to make contact with in . . . in Hong Kong, or Lantao?"

Duquesne understood immediately.

"No," he answered curtly.

# CHAPTER SEVEN

THE TAXI DROPPED DUQUESNE at Kai Tak Airport, and he walked into the terminal with his eyes riveted in front of him, as a child will keep them, in the hope that those whom he does not see cannot see him.

The clerk took his ticket and glanced at his passport; James Gleason, accountant, from Melbourne. His ticket was taken, his bag was put on to the luggage conveyor-belt and his boarding pass given to him without comment. Duquesne, who had timed his arrival to coincide with the main rush of passengers, went straight to the immigration-desk, where again there was no delay or questioning.

The officials at the security check unexpectedly asked for his passport again. Duquesne held his breath as a list was consulted. The Chinese official went deliberately from page to page, glancing back several times at the passport. This new passport bore a Hong Kong entry stamp dated a week before. Duquesne thought the official's face would always remain in his mind.

Then, incuriously, the man handed back the passport and boarding card and looked to the next passenger. Duquesne was trembling. But he knew that for all official purposes he had now left Hong Kong.

In Singapore he had a three-hour wait for his flight, which left at midnight. Already under the influence of the carving up of time by air travel, Duquesne put his mind to sleep—his nerves, too, as far as he could—and pretended he was indeed a clerk from Melbourne, off on holiday.

The Singapore Airlines plane was groaning with passengers. Duquesne waited till after Bangkok, then drank two whiskies, ate the meal provided and took a sleeping pill. He slept through Bombay, but was fully awake in Athens, where it was not quite dawn. Finally, in the cold light of morning, came Heathrow, huge and mechanical, swallowing up the hundreds and thousands pouring in from its three terminals.

At the Royal Court Hotel in Sloane Square the receptionist frowned and said his room would not be ready until 1 p.m. She asked for payment in advance as it was for only one night. Lightheaded, Duquesne laughed, then paid and left his new suitcase, but kept his briefcase. He took a taxi to the post office off St. Martin's Lane and collected his small parcel of seeds posted to himself from Canberra.

London then became for him a pub in the King's Road, where he tasted again that comfortable security and the half-forgotten pub smells. Later he ate a meal of beef and potatoes washed down with two pints of beer. By three o'clock he was in bed in the Royal Court, deep down in the utter stupor that jet travel finally extorts.

# PART THREE

# HARVEST

# CHAPTER ONE

Leaving the Alitalia flight at Pisa, Duquesne picked up a Hertz car which had been reserved for him. It happened to be an Alfa, and driving it he immediately felt better. It was clever of the Russians to afford him this breather, this period of lone travel. Had Irina told them he liked cars?

A little lightheaded from travel, Duquesne was not yet competent to assess the full realities of the situation. At no stage had he erred, but at no stage had he done right. He was uncertain now if he was a victim of others, or himself a traitor. But for the moment he could only pursue a parallel track to the main stream of his problems.

Once past Grosseto, the Via Aurelia ran in sight of the sea. Already summer proclaimed itself in sheen on the turquoise of the sea. Umbrella-pines spread their intricacies of shade and light on the road. The Alfa ran on sweetly and swiftly. He stopped for lunch in Orbetello, a cramped little town looking from its walls to Argentario, across the lagoon. The past assailed him. Nearby was Ansedonia, where he and Meg and Jane had holidayed once for a month. They had lived in a villa and watched the sun set over Argentario. They had swum in the mornings and explored the golden countryside in the afternoon.

On an impulse he drove by Cosa, the old Roman frontier outpost, and thought of hours they had passed within its massive limestone walls, saw the waving asphodel and acanthus, and smelt the scented sunburned grass. In the quiet hours after lunch he had taught his daughter Jane to read. A spasm of loneliness and regret attacked him momentarily. What if things had gone right and they had stayed together? He wouldn't be alone now.

Resisting the temptation to follow the Via Aurelia in to Rome, he turned off to Casal Palocco, towards Ostia. The address he had been given in Viale Alessandro Magno was a large villa in spacious grounds surrounded partly by a high wall, partly by an impenetrable cypress-hedge. The gate was opened to him by a tall, immensely strong man of military aspect, with clumsy features. His face shone with fat, curiously furrowed in unexpected places as though by old wounds, and his eyes were a soft liquid brown. Speaking English imperfectly but adequately, he introduced himself as Zubkovich.

"You had good journey?" he asked, and held out his hand.

"Good? It went smoothly, without detection."

"This we know." Zubkovich nodded several times gravely. He helped Duquesne carry his scant luggage to the house and added: "The car I can deliver back to Hertz tomorrow."

"Oh, no, I'll keep the car," Duquesne casually interposed. "I'll need it while I'm here, especially living out on the Via Cristoforo Colombo."

The man stopped and said heavily: "It is better to go out little, very little."

"I'll keep it," repeated Duquesne calmly. "Nothing is more inconspicuous than an Alfa in Italy."

Regarding the matter closed, he carried his own bag upstairs and into his bedroom. The house was square, with big box-like rooms and high ceilings, pleasantly and slightly overfurnished in the better bourgeois style. Duquesne's room had been a boy's room, and its wallpaper bore elegant daggers and swords. From the window he looked over concealed rooftops and pines and eucalypts to a flaming band of cloud that flashed and changed to gold and pink under his eyes. In a few minutes darkness had fallen.

Downstairs he and Zubkovich were served dinner by a red-cheeked peasant girl with a good-humoured and expansive smile. She was nervous with Zubkovich and clumsy in her efforts to please. When Duquesne addressed her in Italian, even though it was rather rusty, she smiled at him gratefully. They ate pasta in brodo and thin veal steaks. They drank a great deal of heavy Barolo, and afterwards Zubkovich brought out a bottle of vodka. With the drink Zubkovich became more animated, and they began to talk of London, where Zubkovich had spent two years with the Russian embassy, then of England generally. Inevitably they talked of current strike problems, tentatively on Duquesne's side, enthusiastically on Zubkovich's.

"A country decadent and ripe for revolution," he declared. "Look at the wages of their workers, the lowest in the Western world. Look at their productivity, consequently."

"The two are inextricably bound, indeed," agreed Duquesne, watching him.

"Ground under the heel of their capitalist bosses," declared Zubkovich, and his big fist slapped suddenly down on the table. Duquesne started involuntarily. The gesture seemed to belong to a poor film. Suspecting that these weary platitudes were being brought out with him alone in view, Duquesne excused himself early and rose.

"I'll take a walk and clear my head," he said. "I've been sitting for two days now."

"We will walk in the garden. I shall turn on the lights," said Zubkovich.

"Eh? Oh, it's too damp in the garden. I'll stroll down the road."

"In Casal Palocco are many foreigners," stated Zubkovich. "You have worked in Rome before. It is too possible you meet them while you walk."

"I'll put on dark glasses. It's a favourite Italian dodge," grinned Duquesne. "They love wearing them in the dark."

"This walk I do not like. I accompany you." Zubkovich slapped the table again and got laboriously to his feet.

"All right," said Duquesne, giving it up.

Outside under the mimosa trees they met only Alsatian dogs bounding along, their owners in tow. Duquesne walked as quickly as he could, enjoying the fact that Zubkovich had difficulty in keeping up with him. When they got back he went thankfully to bed and slept for ten hours.

It was the beginning of a strange period. Duquesne had agreed to avoid Rome until the meeting began. Zubkovich recognised the extent of Duquesne's boredom and restlessness, and they drove into the country each morning. He also fetched English newspapers for him from town. But Duquesne thought these concessions were backed by mistrust and even hostility on the part of Zubkovich, whose convictions were so much at war with his present surroundings. He sensed in him great reserves of outrage, suppressed rumblings of anger.

The Russian did his best, however. The second morning he looked at Duquesne quickly and said: "There is a game we could play, to pass time, if you wish it." He produced a couple of ping-pong bats. "There is a table in the basement."

The idea of this ponderous man playing ping-pong was incongruous, but Duquesne was pleased. He had been a stylish player as a youth. Zubkovich played with enormous concentration, and considerable agility for such a heavy man. He beat Duquesne roundly the first morning and beamed his pleasure. The second morning Duquesne's old dexterity began to come back, and he won the first game. Then another, in quick succession. The third game Zubkovich played with almost painful attention and seriousness, the little grunts he made after each shot the only sound apart from the clicking of the balls. Duquesne relaxed a little, and Zubkovich just managed to win.

Zubkovich threw down his bat and said: "You were playing left-handed last game. Why?"

"I used to play left-handed sometimes. I'm not ambidextrous, though—far from it."

"Why, then, do you do it?"

Duquesne laughed. "Hell, just to make the game more even."

They fell into a sort of routine. Driving in the morning, lunch at Casal Palocco, papers at three, table tennis at five. Then drinks and dinner, and more drinking. Then walking. Then bed.

Rivalry took many forms, Duquesne reflected. That he and Zubkovich should indulge their growing dislike of each other in competition at the ping-pong table seemed unlikely behaviour for two grown men.

On the afternoon of the fifth day, Duquesne beat Zubkovich five times in succession.

"We have one more game!" The Russian was sweating.

Duquesne assented.

At twenty all, Zubkovich served a sliced ball which Duquesne misjudged. On his next service, Duquesne hit a clean winner to the very edge of the table. Twenty-one all. Two men, tensely opposed in the semi-underground games room. The world outside had ceased to exist for the present. They continued, and Zubkovich caught Duquesne serving left-handed. He threw his bat down on the floor with such force it splintered.

"I have asked you not to do this! I demand . . . another game."

"I'll play right-handed," said Duquesne grimly. "Get yourself a good bat. You'll need it."

He played with complete concentration and won again, easily this time. He appreciated the almost audible effort Zubkovich made not to lose his temper completely.

That afternoon Zubkovich left him alone. When they came to have dinner, Zubkovich was clearly half-drunk, and twice he upset his wine.

Afterwards they listened to the BBC overseas news. There followed a talk on the strikes of the previous two years, the worst in England since the General Strike of 1926. The speaker talked of the time when pickets stopped supplies to hospitals and decided which sick persons should be admitted.

Zubkovich began shouting.

"It is only time before the revolution—in England as well."

"You don't really think that communists could overthrow English democracy, do you, Zubkovich?" asked Duquesne curiously.

"Ha! Democracy will overthrow itself! English is going down, down, down!" He brought his hand down *slap* on the table.

"Of course, in your country, strikes are forbidden," Duquesne said enticingly, and sat back and waited.

"We to whom the future belongs, we must be . . . socially united! We cannot afford the luxury of disputes, as in England."

Duquesne said mildly: "You miss the point, you know, Zubkovich. England is a country with a great tradition of freedom. It is working out all sorts of tensions and contradictions. It is thanks to this tradition of meeting and striking and arguing that they work this out. Grievances are not crushed beneath the surface to fester away and lead on to the sort of things that Solzhenitsyn, for instance, writes of."

Fury suddenly seized Zubkovich, turning his face white, bringing him to his feet. He kicked his chair over and roared: "You will not speak of that madman and traitor!"

Duquesne looked at him in silence for a moment. Then, with the feeling that he was taking a necessary, even inevitable step, said: "Oh, I'll speak of whom I like, Zubkovich. You don't understand very much about the English, I'm afraid. It's a free society, which yours is most definitely not." He had opened the flood-gates and sat back to wait for the onrush of the waters. "Whatever happens in England . . ." he began.

"What happens in England is that the workers will join together and there will come the dictatorship of the proletariat," shouted Zubkovich. He stood over Duquesne, his eyes bulging, his great hand crashing down on the table.

"Oh, for Christ's sake," said Duquesne wearily and deliberately. "All this bloody tired old patter. You've ruled by fear for nearly sixty years and the workers haven't had a say in things yet."

"You will not say this!" *Crash* went the fist.

"On the contrary"—Duquesne got casually to his feet, with a great feeling of surprise that it was happening—"I'll say what I bloody well like to anyone."

With an exclamation Zubkovich took hold of Duquesne by the shoulder. His hand closed like a vice. His breath, reeking of drink, hit Duquesne's face. Duquesne felt the wall behind him as he was edged back.

"Don't make a fool of yourself," he said coldly.

Zubkovich's heavy mouth was open, edged with spittle, and Duquesne could see his very white teeth and his very red tongue. Then Zubkovich began to shake him, like a dog. Zubkovich's face receded some inches, and Duquesne knew he was going to be hit. Duquesne's knee went up in a vicious thrust, and he got Zubkovich in the genitals. Zubkovich's grip on his shoulder loosened. Duquesne immediately hit him in the throat with his fist. Zubkovich staggered back, slipped on the marble floor and crashed down on his back.

Duquesne stood getting his breath back for a moment. The Russian lay like a stone where he had fallen. Duquesne lifted Zubkovich's head and banged it down on the marble floor twice for good measure. He checked that Zubkovich was still breathing. Then he hurried out of the room.

# CHAPTER TWO

IT WAS 9.30. Duquesne ran downstairs to the telephone and unplugged it. Then he opened the kitchen door. The maid Giovanna, clashing dishes in the sink, had heard nothing. Popular music blared forth deafeningly from a little radio, and Giovanna sang with it. Duquesne thought she sang for him. She blushed as he entered.

"Giovanna, può aiutarmi?" He smiled as engagingly as he could. "I must make some calls urgently to Australia. This phone doesn't work. Could I come home with you now and phone from your house?"

She was clearly dumbfounded. Duquesne said quickly: "Your husband won't mind, will he? I know he'll be there. I'll pay the calls and give you ten thousand lire more for the trouble."

She agreed. He could follow her Vespa in the car.

She lived in the little village of Acilia, perched on a ridge several kilometres away. Duquesne followed her with some difficulty down the main street, clogged with cars, and over the railway line, down a dark country road.

Her home was a flat in a half-finished block. Her young fat husband was seated at the kitchen table spooning up the soup she had left ready for him to heat. In no time, Duquesne was closed in the "best" room, putting his first call through to Jerry. It was 8 a.m. in Australia. He could not have timed it better.

"They haven't found Temple," said Jerry grimly. "I've practically camped down in your house the last two weekends, and there has not been a sign of life. They haven't the remotest idea where he is, it's obvious. Silkin agrees."

Duquesne's relief was so great he could find no words at first. He managed finally: "That's great."

"Silkin wants you to phone Woods at this number, 328476, in Melbourne. It's a Mont Albert line, tell the operator. Woods is at home right now, because we have been keeping in touch, the three of us, in case you should phone one of us."

When he rang off, Duquesne sat there at the table, his head in his hands, oblivious to his surroundings. A fierce battle swayed back and forth within him, old loyalties and attitudes against personal pride and ambition.

After some minutes he picked up the phone and dialled the operator once more. He was told there was a twenty-minute delay. While he waited he tried two hotels he knew in Rome for a bed that night, without success. Then he remembered that from Australia he had booked a room for himself and Irina at a hotel in the Aventino area. He had booked it for a week beginning that night. He rang the Hotel Santa Prisca to say he would arrive late.

Then he went out to the kitchen and talked to the pair there. He was faintly embarrassed to be there, to be so conspicuously a nuisance, but there was no help for it. Giovanna's large red hands set a tiny cup of coffee before him with absurd care. The husband's glance avoided him. He certainly wanted to go to bed.

When Woods came through Duquesne said: "I'm speaking on a hundred-per-cent-safe line. Are you?"

"Oh, yes, I think so." On the telephone Woods's voice was over-refined and irritating. But he went straight to the point.

"Silkin found out what one of those keys of Temple's opened. It was the key of a compartment concealed in the kitchen in Temple's Sydney flat. The kitchen, for God's sake." Woods managed to sound affronted, even at that distance.

Duquesne went cold. Woods, too, must know of Dick's death, of course.

"There were two things in the compartment," Woods said softly and clearly. "One was a tape. The voices haven't been authenticated yet, but there seems no doubt that they are genuine. Temple for some reason taped a telephone talk he had with the American Ambassador in Canberra. The Ambassador refers openly to the uranium deal and its link-up with the suppression of your wheat."

"He does that! On a tape-recording?" Duquesne was taken by surprise.

"Oh, yes. The second thing in the compartment was a draft of a report which Temple either had sent to Washington or was preparing to send. In it he assesses how far you and several others who know or might suspect the real story of the wheat-uranium connection may be trusted to keep quiet about it."

"And he had decided I couldn't be trusted?" Duquesne asked.

"He considered you highly unreliable, but—as he nicely put it—too wet behind the ears politically to guess what was going on. But all the same he thought you could be a nuisance."

Woods laughed encouragingly. Duquesne did not respond. A surge of anger ran through him. They were all so bloody knowledgeable about the realities of the rotten world of politics, while he was an innocent. He forced calm on himself. Temple might not have been wrong in his assessment, but Temple's superior knowledge was no use to him now.

"Go on," Duquesne said grimly.

"I wonder if you would be prepared to make a statement at the meeting, Doctor. I think that the evidence we hold, together with a statement by you, would enable the Opposition to insist that the Governor-General dissolves Parliament. We can be quite sure what the result of a general election would be in those circumstances. But it must be a full statement. I think"—Woods might have been expounding an interesting proposition to a university seminar—"that it must all come out into the light of day, or all remain hidden. It depends entirely on you, and no one will try to force your hand for a moment. It is not a risk which anyone else has the slightest right to encourage you to take."

"Yes." Duquesne was terse. His head was pounding. "Go on."

"Let me restate the situation as I see it. If you choose to talk, you may rely on our producing the evidence in question. I see no reason why we should fail to blow the Government sky high but, as you know, we are dealing with a man who is a master of the unexpected. And you personally could well lose out on all counts. I don't think that you will, but it could happen."

After a pause, Woods added: "If you want to think this over further, by all means do so. Oh, one other thing. If you do speak out, it would be much more effective for our operation here if some solid indication were given by you first that you so intend. I would suggest an advance statement to the press, which could hit the headlines here as soon as possible. Phone me back at four this afternoon. From four onwards. That's six a.m. tomorrow for you."

"I'll do that."

"Oh, and, Doctor"—Woods's voice was soft, and gentler than ever—"let me say that if I were you I should feel scared as hell. And I want to tell you that if you do decide to speak you'll have the profound admiration of a number of people here whose opinion is probably well worth having."

When he rang off, Duquesne, on an impulse, put a third call in, to Sydney this time. But when, quite soon, the call was answered it was not Meg's slow voice on the line, but, he realised with a glad leap of his heart, Jane's.

"Oh, Daddy, how perfectly super to hear you. When are you coming to Sydney? Where are you?" The squeal of delight was unmistakable. "It's a holiday here, and I'm at Mummy's. I've got loads of homework, and it's beastly. . . ." After the call was over he sat exhausted. Giovanna, tiptoeing in, caught him wet-eyed.

"Niente," he explained, smiling at her. "La figlia questa volta, lo sai? My daughter this time."

Nothing could have pleased them more, and as he left he carried with him Giovanna's delighted expression as she nodded to her husband: "Era la *figlia.* Quant'era emozionato, hai visto?"

An hour later he crunched up the driveway from the Via Marmorata and parked the Alfa in front of the Santa Prisca. The night porter was unenthusiastic, but stirred himself to lead Duquesne to a first-floor room with a pretty tiled floor, a balcony and a double bed which promised comfort. A good hotel, Duquesne thought. Twenty minutes later the porter surprised him by bringing up a letter which had been awaiting Duquesne for some days. It was from the Rome correspondent of a major London paper and requested an interview. The letter was signed Stephen Crane. His brother in Hong Kong had mentioned that Duquesne would very likely be attending the United Nations conference in Rome. An enterprising fellow, Crane's brother. He must have phoned every good-class hotel in town. Duquesne found himself laughing. You wanted a news splash—you got a reporter. Was his luck turning?

He sank into a chair and resolutely prepared himself for the long inward struggle before him, wondering how many men ever brought to the forefront of their consciousness, ever dared explore their strengths and weaknesses, their motives and values, stripped of the handy code of behaviour imposed by familiar routine and an assured place in a particular country's scheme of things.

There were many things he wanted to know about himself, and he hoped he could find the answers. He wished now he had never insisted on the United Nations meeting, that he had told Menshikov he would go straight to Russia. Rome had only confused him. Values tended to slip and slide in this soft Mediterranean air. Sharpness of purpose, intensity of resolve wavered. Though Casal Palocco should have been safe enough, only a few days had been enough to eat away at his resolution. Menshikov had been superb, but now his memory was blunted by travel, by the chopping up of time, by the humourless fanaticism of Zubkovich—a curious choice of the Russians at this critical time. Duquesne grinned at the thought of their scuffle, which actually had nothing to do with his present problems. Except that Zubkovich was so bloody strong Duquesne should now by rights be dead. Somehow he had jumped over that fact without getting scared by it. He had not had the time, and perhaps he, too, had been rather drunk.

Jane on the telephone. Oh Christ. In Russia would he ever see Jane again? They had told him he was free to have his family with him. What the hell did he want? He wanted to develop his discovery. He wanted Jane. He wanted peace. He wanted freedom.

The Russian offer had attraction as the way of science against the hedging and the obstacles of Australia. He wanted to be loyal to his discovery, but that discovery had been made in a certain setting, in a certain country, which had furnished him the means. Loyalty to that country was inbred in him. But science was universal.

He had found and liked in Menshikov a largeness of spirit and ideas. But was it all a blind? The Russian offer had come when all else had failed, come immediately after his rejection by his own country. At the time it had seemed not only opportune, but also, clothed in

Menshikov's words, an honourable opportunity to continue his work without regard to political colour or national loyalties. One short week in Rome and the outlines of the picture were shifting, ill-defined and fluid as though seen underwater. A thousand doubts were at work in him now, and in this supremely human Roman setting life in Russia —Menshikov even—was no longer quite real.

He did not think he had been dishonest. But, if he had been able to smother his aversion to communism in Hong Kong, why could he not do so now in Rome? Because in Hong Kong he had had no alternative if he wanted to leave a free man. Had he, then, so distorted the truth? He remembered his enormous relief when Jerry had told him Dick's body had not been found. Underneath everything, then, was his terribly deep-seated desire to remain in the West. It was what he really wanted, if it were possible. Somehow, then, he had to reconcile his acceptance of the Russian offer, when it was expedient, when accepting it meant getting out of Hong Kong and not being bustled back to Australia a virtual prisoner, with his decision to reject it now—now that the chance offered itself of speaking out at the United Nations meeting and of exposing a major instance of cynical political opportunism, where the rich looked after their own and the hell with the others. Did expediency explain his own actions? But no, it was not more than a tiny part of the truth.

He believed—or he wanted to believe—that his overriding ambition was to make sure that the developing countries were not deprived of his discovery. It was very much at the heart of his decision to speak out now at the meeting. It was also something else. He had suddenly got to the point of defiance. He was going to be his own man.

He lay back exhausted. He had tried to be very hard on himself and very fair. And he wondered if any one of all those who had dealt with him recently had applied to themselves this sort of painstaking and rigorous test.

At three in the morning he fell into a troubled sleep. His decision was taken—once more. Whatever awaited him now, he would reject the offer of Menshikov and tomorrow he would inform the Russians.

# CHAPTER THREE

HE WOKE AT NINE with a start to bright sunlight and all the little insistent noises of an old hotel—running water gushing through pipes and outlets, steps re-echoing, crockery clattering and, from the Via Marmorata below, the grind of the traffic. Someone was hammering somewhere, each metallic rap a nail in Duquesne's head. He wanted to fall now into a deep sound sleep and have ten more hours of oblivion.

Woods. Phone Woods. He groped, tiredly, for consciousness. Should have phoned Woods at six. Feverishly he pawed for the telephone and told the hotel operator to call Australia, panicking as he heard the girl's indolent voice. It was only a small hotel, and it was the hour of the *conversazione.*

*"E urgente, molto urgente,* I stay here in my room to wait for it. You must call urgently." He was loud and authoritative. She might, then, bestir herself.

He bathed with the bathroom door open, dressed, called for coffee. In a curious state now, feverish yet detached, he jotted down notes for his exposé at the meeting.

Woods, when he came on the line finally, sounded elated behind the softness when Duquesne said: "I've decided to play the sacrificial lamb and talk."

"It's good news. I admire your decision and your courage to act on it. We have little time now. *What*—it is important I know—*what* will you say, fairly exactly? Have you decided that?"

"It will be a technical résumé of experiments and results to date, of course. I have this with me now, together with samples of the seed."

"Yes, yes." Woods's voice was soft as silk now. "But the background? We need to be *quite* sure, here, of what you intend."

"Have you a pencil? There'll be no insinuations, no rhetoric. It will be a pure statement of fact, and I've written it down to make sure I've got it right. In brief, as a scientist, I am putting my loyalties first to science. The work on this discovery has come to a virtual end in Australia. I am not satisfied it should be so, because I consider it too valuable—or so it could prove—to over half the world's population. If the testing is kept secret, it means, in reality, either suppressing the discovery or delaying any widescale use for years. It is at the stage where it needs worldwide testing under a range of conditions.

"I have therefore decided to break the silence imposed on me by my own country. Far from being able to go ahead with my work, I have been spied on, followed, impeded in every way, and my movements have been restricted. My home has been searched. A test crop was deliberately burned.

"The wheat is there. If international testing is done in an efficient and scientific manner, no underdeveloped country will be misled. The uncertainties and risks of possible failure must be made very obvious.

"The wheat is a discovery eminently worthy of urgent attention for the benefit of the world. I consider this UN meeting—an international meeting on grains attended by scientists—is the right and proper venue to make my report.

"I want the meeting to be in no doubt, however, that my report is being delivered without the consent of the Australian government. But it seems that, unless I do take such action, the wheat could remain forever unknown and untried.

"I have nothing but the most profound admiration and respect for the head of my department in Australia, Sir John Doughty. However, his hands are tied. Secrecy was imposed on him from above. I am therefore breaking faith with him and deliberately breaking the promise I made to my own Prime Minister that I would not reveal the discovery, and I do this because I consider that I was deliberately deceived. I think the intention was either not to develop the wheat or to delay it until years and years of valuable time had been wasted. I was told that testing would be stepped up, but within Australia. It was not so. Two countries, for motives of self-interest, intend to suppress this discovery, and another has attempted to appropriate it by buying me and my services.

"However, this is not the proper place for the hearing of such a case. It will immediately be fought out in Australia, as is right and just, but I have no compunction in mentioning the background here, as it is so soon to be made public." Duquesne stopped. "That will be the essence of my statement at the meeting."

"Yes, yes, it will more than suffice." Woods's voice was softer than ever. "Shall I ring you tomorrow? Or you me? I think we should arrange to phone at a certain hour each day from now on. Now, your advance statement to the press. . . ."

"I am about to arrange an interview with the representative in Rome of a London paper. Don't worry"—Duquesne's lip curled—"I shall say enough to commit myself *quite* irrevocably."

"Splendid, Doctor, splendid. And now we'll go to work this end, fast." Woods purred the words, and they bade each other goodbye.

When Duquesne put the receiver down he was trembling. He suffered the maid to do his bed and slosh a wet rag round the bathroom floor. Then he sat down at the absurd little hotel writing table and drafted a long letter to Menshikov in which he tried to present an honest picture of the mental struggle which had led to his rejection of the Russian offer. Then he wrote a formal letter to the Russian Embassy, which arranged to repay the amount of his travel expenses from Hong Kong to Rome. He was glad an official contract had not been signed.

Lastly, he rang the reporter and promised to meet him in the lobby of the Hassler at the top of the Spanish Steps at three that afternoon.

"My brother in Hong Kong told me that you were an old FAO hand," said the younger Crane, across a bar table in the Hassler. He was an elongated thin Crane, with the same keen eyes.

"Some years ago I was at the FAO." Duquesne had been carried along for some minutes on the suggestive wave of Crane's preparatory patter, and was amused at his efficiency. He was wondering if *mediamonger* was a word yet. And then awareness of his own precarious situation swept over him once more, bringing the familiar tension in his gut.

"What do you think about the future contribution of plant breeding to solving the food problem, Dr. Duquesne?"

Gratefully, Duquesne recognised the lead-in.

"There is far greater scope than is generally realised," he replied. He went on to sketch out some of the major discoveries of recent decades, stressing Borlaug's innovations. Not only were they deserving, but it was one name that reporters all knew. It made them feel safe.

"But in my own work," Duquesne said, "I have learned that the plant scientist is only one actor on a well-filled stage. He may think he knows what the play is all about and what he himself should do and say. It is all too frequently not so."

"Uh-*huh.* Keeping things under wraps?"

"Exactly."

"Can you cite actual examples?"

"I intend to," Duquesne replied grimly.

"When?"

"At the United Nations meeting which begins here next week at the headquarters of the Food and Agriculture Organisation."

"As an Australian representative?"

"I shall attend in my personal capacity and speak only for myself. And for millions of hungry people who need not be in that condition if knowledge which is available were translated into action. Knowledge that I myself have been privileged to contribute to," said Duquesne deliberately. "In brief, there are plants which could revolutionise food prospects in the poor countries of the tropics but which are being deliberately kept secret."

Crane's eyes gleamed. This was good stuff. He could already see the headline: " 'SECOND GREEN REVOLUTION SUPPRESSED,' SAYS AUSTRALIAN SCIENTIST." It would continue: "Leading Australian plant scientist, Dr. Jack Duquesne, alleged to our special correspondent Stephen Crane in Rome yesterday that vital breakthroughs were being deliberately suppressed." Big news, a scoop. Real news was scarce at present.

"You appreciate, Dr. Duquesne, that what you say may not seem credible?"

"Perhaps not. But it happens."

"You are surely not speaking of Australia, Doctor? Australia is such a leader in agricultural science and its application."

Duquesne was startled. Was this question just chance or did the reporter know? He thought not, but it was a good opportunity to bring the kettle closer to boiling.

"Well, for instance, in 1977 evidence was reported in Australia of administrative suppression in New South Wales of wheat varieties capable of increasing yields by ten per cent."

Crane was interested but a little disappointed. Ten per cent wasn't much but, still, the actual figure need not be quoted.

"Can I check what you say?" he smiled. "Reporters also respect evidence."

Duquesne immediately cited the full reference to the meeting of the Australian society concerned.

The reporter stared, impressed. His brother had said that Duquesne had to be taken seriously, that there was a real story in the man. He encouraged Duquesne to talk of the possibilities of plant breeding, of constraints and how they had been overcome in quotable instances, of the scientific community and their loyalty to their profession. A pity that Duquesne would not talk directly of what might come out at the United Nations meeting next week, but he did hint that two other countries besides Australia had subordinated innovations in plant breeding to other considerations. He had said enough.

Crane's thoughts raced on. "While women and children die of hunger, Australia holds back on new food plants. Australian scientist, Dr. Jack Duquesne . . ." The article practically wrote itself to feature on the front page of the eminent London paper the next morning. A careful reader might think that the article was as short on facts as it was long on suggestion, but undoubtedly it was readable. People would keep an eye on revelations at the United Nations meeting next week.

Crane admired his own skill as he reread the telex copy the following morning and drank his cappuccino at Piazza del Popolo. The Australian Ambassador in Rome was less happy, as he was stopped from leaving for an unofficial afternoon's golf at Olgiata. He cursed and reached for the phone.

# CHAPTER FOUR

TOWARDS MID-AFTERNOON on Friday, Robert Weaver stood lost in thought in the corridor outside the Ambassador's door in the United States Embassy, Rome. A typist, stepping briskly by, greeted him familiarly, but he looked straight through her and unseeing walked automatically towards his own office. Then he began a similar jerky and interrupted promenade up and down his spacious room, a room more luxurious than a relatively junior official might be expected to rate.

He was immersed in a delicate interpretation of a totally unexpected and lengthy talk with his Ambassador following the Ambassador's receipt of an urgent top-secret communication from Washington. His cogitation over, Weaver unlocked a filing cabinet and extracted some papers. Glancing over them, he dialled the operator and said: "I want to speak to—ah—the co-ordinating secretary of the UN meeting on grains starting at FAO next Monday. I don't know who it is."

When he was connected he heard the man say: "You know I'm afraid I can't tell you anything about Dr. Duquesne. He seems to be much in demand. It's the third call I've had on his account. He is attending the meeting, but he wrote that he would make his own accommodation arrangements. Perhaps he is staying with friends. I don't know whether he would be in Rome yet. Yes, I'll get in touch with you if I hear."

Weaver sat motionless for a moment, his eyes veiled. His thoughts were on a young colleague who had lost his life in Australia several weeks before. He had learned from a friend in Washington, D.C., what had happened in the helicopter incident. And now Dick Temple, too, was missing, presumed dead. He lifted the telephone receiver again, but thought better about it. Rising, he made his way out to the street. Walking up to the corner of Via Boncompagni, he turned left and strolled along under the trees until he reached a small bar where he often took coffee. Luckily he was able to enjoy both American and Italian coffee—an accomplishment shared by few of his fellow-countrymen. He drank a cappuccino and approached the telephone. At that hour the bar was empty except for a German couple breathing into their beers at the far end. Weaver thoughtfully lifted the receiver, inserted a *gettone* and made his call. He listened, nodded with satisfaction and repeated: "It's good of you. In an hour's time, then, in the piazza in front of San Pietro in Montorio?"

Some fifteen minutes before then he parked his car a good distance away and walked down to the little-known piazza. It was deserted except for two Spanish nuns who came up the steps leading from the Via di Porta San Pancrazio. They went through the archway into the cloister, and Weaver followed them, looking, with them, on Bramante's Tempietto. It meant nothing to him, this small unassuming structure in faded mustard wash, though he knew that it was supposed to represent the apex of building during the high Renaissance. So he returned to the piazza and from the wall allowed his eyes to wander over the rooftops of Trastevere to the statues on the great basilica of St. John Lateran, and beyond to the thin blue line of the Alban Hills.

Then he turned round to see Zubkovich walking towards him, enormous and out of place. Weaver, slim and of middle height, of a deceptively gentle demeanour, went to meet him.

Zubkovich owed a debt to Weaver. By a far chance, Weaver had helped him one night in a Rome nightclub. Zubkovich had been very drunk. The waiter had addressed Zubkovich contemptuously in German and given him a bill of absurd size. Zubkovich had risen and shouted. The waiter had remained firm that he should pay. Zubkovich had hit him. The man had gone down bleeding.

The manager appeared. In no time, as if by magic, a *carabiniere* as well. Zubkovich, protesting, gave the man his diplomatic card. The man took it by the corner, glanced at it, screwed it up, and threw it under the table.

Then it was that Weaver, suspicious, had come forward and asked the man for his identification. The *carabiniere* had blustered, and

Weaver, who had an intimate knowledge of Italian, knew from their side-exchange that the policeman was a fake. Weaver took advantage of their momentary hesitation. He dropped several 100,000-lire notes on the table, took hold of Zubkovich's arm firmly and marched him outside. Then he put Zubkovich into his car and drove him home.

Weaver had not wasted this chance contact. He had followed it up only two weeks later when he had divulged to Zubkovich the efforts of a refugee from the German Democratic Republic to play the double agent to their two countries. He guessed that Moscow had been told of the unidentifiable body in the Tiber before the Rome police had found it.

Together they strolled along the wall under the gawky palm trees. From below, the rumble of the city drifted up to mingle with the screech and moan of gears as vehicles changed down to swoop round the nearby fountain.

Now Weaver began speaking.

"There is a man called Jack Duquesne in Rome at the moment." He did not miss Zubkovich's immediate stiffening, the alarm in his eyes. "He is going to prove a nuisance to us."

Weaver paused and tried his luck.

"Perhaps also to you?"

Zubkovich, looking down on Weaver like a bear regarding a cobra, grunted some sort of assent. Weaver could not know that he had been combing Rome for Duquesne all that morning.

"I can't find him," said Weaver simply. "He's here, but he's gone to ground. He is due to attend a UN meeting at FAO."

There was a pause.

"I may look for him," declared Zubkovich.

Weaver looked into space once more, over to the Alban Hills.

"This is one of the times when my country must not itself take any direct steps to impede Duquesne from attending this meeting and speaking his mind. However, we would be relieved if he were not able to do so."

Zubkovich was breathing noisily, and his hand went instinctively to his throat, which, could Weaver have known it, still throbbed from the punishing blow of Duquesne.

He said: "Is it only this meeting? Perhaps you wish him not to speak at *any* more meetings." His beautiful liquid brown eyes gazed into Weaver's.

Weaver said casually: "There does seem to be a lot of unnecessary talking at meetings nowadays."

Zubkovich's face seemed to swell above Weaver. He put out a hand as though to pat him consolingly on the shoulder, but then it dropped to his side.

"I may look for him," he repeated. "Yes. Then we meet here again. This is a good place to meet."

Weaver watched him walking off solitary and huge against the incongruous background of a throng of Italian schoolgirls who suddenly materialised in the piazza, laughing and calling to each other like a crowd of bright chattering birds. Weaver shivered, then he consciously relaxed and switched off the miniature recorder in the additional inside pocket. He assumed that Zubkovich had done the same as soon as he was out of sight.

# CHAPTER FIVE

"I WANT TO BRING the Government down," said Woods quietly, almost dreamily, pacing up and down in Holmes's office in the Australian Labour Party's headquarter in Canberra.

Holmes, the Opposition leader, glanced at Woods and away again.

"You won't, though, David." He slapped his hand on the table and nearly upset his beer. "Not this crowd, not for a long, long time."

"Blantyre is leading this country into an age of quite appallingly crude conservatism," said Woods, still on the same quiet note.

Holmes shrugged.

"Australians *are* conservative. They feel safe with the Libs." He was silent for a moment and then added: "Blantyre is *formidable.* He kicks difficulties away regardless. Look at the suggestion last month that he might have tried to influence a Minister giving evidence before a public enquiry. It might have been explosive. It should have been. What happens? 'Rubbish,' says Blantyre. In two weeks the thing is forgotten. Scandal hardly touches him."

"Perhaps it hasn't been bad enough scandal," said Woods, smiling.

Holmes looked enquiringly at him, but Woods merely said: "I want a government whose appeal is not just to businessmen and big farmers and mining tycoons. I want a government that has regard also for intangibles and is not afraid of ideals, such as influencing world opinion against nuclear development, or conserving our environment."

"Instead of which we deliberately invite exploitation by the outside world." Holmes was bitter. "There is a very large body of opinion against uranium mining—real opposition. Yet somehow mining goes ahead. You want Aboriginal agreement to mining? Somehow they sign it. No one is fooled that it was a voluntary decision. Everyone knows they were negotiating under duress, that they had no veto over mining under the Lands Rights Act."

"And without their land," said Woods sombrely, "the Aborigines lose their past and their culture."

"Yes, of course," Holmes said impatiently, feeling the conversation less than productive, thinking of the work waiting for him, and feeling he had been angered to no purpose. Woods had asked to see him on a Saturday afternoon, a time normally inviolate. And then he had gone on saying things that had been said a hundred times before. But he had done the party good service in the past.

As Holmes glanced moodily at him, Woods said slyly: "Perhaps I could help."

Holmes was arrested by his tone. He watched Woods take three articles from his briefcase. One was a tiny metal box, one an envelope, the third a large box. He laid them with care on the table. From the large box he took a tape-recorder.

He said very seriously: "Tom, are we alone?"

"Completely."

"Is this room reasonably soundproof?"

"There's no one else here in my whole office."

"Then, I'll play the tape."

Woods inserted it, pressed a key, and an American voice said clearly: "Oh, Temple, I'm sorry to call you, but your line is clean and you shouldn't be seen around the Embassy. There's a complete reversal of instructions about that wheat. Australia has agreed not to go ahead with its development."

There was a pause, and another American voice said, less distinctly: "Oh, is that so? That's very accommodating of them." There was a trace of a laugh in the voice.

"It's not without its advantages for them. For your very private information, they get a fat uranium contract out of it."

"Uranium," said the second American voice thoughtfully. "It's running into a lot of trouble. You know the Aborigines might hold up mining for a long time?"

"We're aware of that," returned the other voice. "But we think that as they'll get at least one hundred million dollars a year out of it, and as the mining companies and the two governments won't have to pay a cent of that—well, everyone who matters should be happy."

"Oh, I see," said the other voice quickly. "Yes, I see."

"You're in Duquesne's house, aren't you?"

"Yes, sir."

"From now on your essential job is to observe *him.* The Australians say he has been talked to and is agreeable, but he might not be reliable, I guess. You'll know how to get into his confidence. If he talks to you, I guess he'll talk to anyone."

"Well, we're getting to be real buddies, you might say."

The sound clicked off.

"Who the bloody hell's that?" demanded Holmes.

"The American Ambassador in Canberra and a CIA agent called Temple," said Woods quietly.

"How the hell did you get that?"

"Never mind how. If you care to use it, your job is to authenticate the voice of the Ambassador."

"What? For Christ's sake, will you tell me what it's all about?"

"Sit down and . . . No, give me a drink first. Yes, Scotch . . . and ice, yes. Now. Duquesne has been developing a wheat he found growing up near the uranium deposits in the Ranger area. The wheat has been found to do exceptionally well in the tropics. Its introduction could transform the food situation in developing countries."

*"What!"*

Woods repeated himself, at some length. Then he continued.

"The U.S. found out about it and, fearful of its impact on their politically powerful and growing wheat exports to developing countries, they pressed Blantyre to suppress the wheat, or at least to postpone its release more or less indefinitely, the U.S. quid pro quo being the lucrative long-term contract announced a short time ago for the purchase of the bulk of Australia's uranium output."

"And royalties?"

"Sure thing. The President is only too glad to have the opportunity for his country to play the benefactor—well publicised, of course—to one of the most primitive groups of peoples anywhere. Of course the U.S. fear strongly that the availability of the wheat would undoubtedly diminish both the prospects and later the actuality of their political clout in many developing countries dependent on grain imports from the U.S."

Holmes was silent, concentrated.

"The U.S. President," went on Woods, "has decided that, despite the current improvement in world oil supplies, energy is still a basic issue and he wants to secure his supplies of uranium. Australia is probably his most reliable foreign source. Look at what is happening in Africa."

"The Government are sitting on this wheat in order to get a uranium contract. . . ." Holmes spoke at last, awe in his voice. "Wheat that can . . . Good Christ. This scientist Duquesne agreed to this?"

"He was sworn to secrecy, but of course he wasn't told of the uranium contract. The Government, too, is apprehensive of the economic impact of this wheat on our own wheat exports and on the wheat-growing areas. Don't forget Blantyre has recently become a wheat farmer himself! And his electorate is largely in a wheat-growing area. Of course, wheat is a tricky crop, and it was emphasised to Duquesne that if his wheat proved a failure in the tropics later on—if it were, for instance, very prone to some disease—it could also ruin a lot of poor devils in the less developed countries, and that Australia would incur all the odium of having introduced it. This was a weighty argument to Duquesne. Blantyre put it to him that the wheat should and would be thoroughly tested first in Australia. But in fact work on it stopped."

Holmes said quietly: "The tape. Is it evidence? Can the identity of the voices be scientifically proved? Without the slightest doubt?"

"Yes. And Duquesne is now in Rome at a meeting of the UN on grains. He has decided, for one reason and another, to give to that meeting a full account of his wheat."

"He *has!*"

"On Monday next," said Woods gently. "If you cared to use the tape, don't you think it would, altogether, be a means of hanging Blantyre by his heels?"

# CHAPTER SIX

THE LEADER of the Australian Opposition sat with his four closest frontbenchers in a party headquarters room. He was tense. The meeting was crucial to the Australian Labour Party.

Holmes's own mind was now made up, but he wanted the support of his colleagues. Three of the four would give it. He hoped he would also get it from old Cawley, who sat at the end of the table. A big, shambling, aging man. Inaccurately shaven, dressed in a suit which his wife, had she still been alive, would have thrown away instantly. A fighter over the years for the political aims he believed in, the most loyal of comrades, but a rugged defender of his own views. In his old age still capable, when he chose, of withering abuse, backed by a powerful mind, which Holmes had seen reduce bright young men to white-faced defeat. Could Holmes carry him, too?

"It's too big a chance to miss," Holmes said, conscious of Jones's toughness, Redpath's angry loyalty, the rigid working-class attitudes of O'Donovan, for whom God was the original trade unionist. "It's big and it should be deadly in its impact. We all know how firmly the present government is entrenched. The Prime Minister may irritate his own colleagues with his authoritarian style. Many people may be angry about the continuing rise in unemployment, particularly of the young. All the same, the Blantyre administration is probably as secure as any in the history of Australia."

Redpath reacted first.

"Let the Liberals lose in Victoria and it might be a different story. That by-election was a disaster!" His ears and neck became very slightly tinged with red. He was usually referred to as "Redneck."

"Nevertheless, Labour lasted only three years, after more than twenty years of being out of power," cut in Holmes firmly. "There's no time to debate it. If we act, we act now. If we leave a decision over till after Duquesne talks on Monday in Rome, Blantyre will jump the gun. My bet is that he'd ride the disclosures; he would overcome them as he overcomes all difficulties, by treading them down."

"That he can hardly do," objected Jones. "If Duquesne likes to give a full account of what the Prime Minister apparently personally extracted from him—a promise to say nothing of the wheat. . . ."

"The Prime Minister can ride it," insisted Holmes. "He'll loom up with that immovable assurance and say yes, of course, Australia has made a world-shaking discovery—rather, it *might* be, but we have to make sure of its possibilities. We don't want to give rise to an abortive Green Revolution. . . ."

"He'll make a fool of that poor bastard." Redneck was vehement. "Duquesne will end up by being the biggest crackpot, the nerviest fool who ever got the wrong end of the stick."

"But the wheat discovery would be safely at the disposal of an international body of scientists." Cawley spoke for the first time.

"And the Right Honourable James Blantyre reap the benefit, unless we get to work." Redneck's ears and neck were now purple. "OK, Tom"—he turned ostentatiously back to Holmes—"I *don't* need convincing. We don't act, Blantyre will ride it. So we act. Now!"

"You might argue that the one thing that does matter in all this is that the developing countries are not deprived of that discovery," Cawley insisted, his eyes on Holmes.

His words jarred on Holmes, who as leader was intent on registering the reactions of the others sensitively. Cawley would always produce an underlayer of truth which, however inopportune, Holmes could not disregard.

"The wheat was very definitely suppressed—crop burned, work stopped?" Cawley asked.

"The Ranger crop was burned immediately after the agreement was made between Blantyre and the U.S. President, yes. It was burned as it was considered too vulnerable to discovery. Duquesne was told that the burning was accidental, but he found later he had been deceived and that his wheat was slated to be suppressed indefinitely, or at least for a damned long time."

"To say nothing of the CIA in it—all along the line," burst out Redneck. "That alone should be blasted sky-high. By God, they've brought down governments before, and this time they'll help to bring another down—a right one."

One part of Holmes's mind appreciated Redneck's unintentional pun.

"As further evidence of CIA involvement", he said, "we have the Sydney reporter, Silkin, who was paid—handsomely—to get information at Ranger about Duquesne's wheat crop. Silkin failed to get samples of the wheat. They then asked him to get details of construction and earth-moving work being carried out at night, the noise of which would give cover to a U.S. helicopter with CIA men on board to collect samples of the wheat. This was before the deal between Blantyre and the President. An Australian security guard tried to shoot the helicopter down. It got away but crashed in the sea. The guard got one of the men, though. The killing was witnessed by an old fellow looking after the wheat crop. He was paid off and sent down to New South Wales. He has been located and would testify."

At his own words Holmes felt righteous comforting anger surge within him.

"It's more than a weapon that can bring the Government down. It so clearly demonstrates their unscrupulous and shortsighted policy and their ruthless search for material benefits." He slid easily into rhetoric. "It takes a callousness of attitude indeed to hold back food from a hungry world to line the pockets of businessmen—Australian and foreign. Our own government, in the few years it had power, made mistakes, but our objectives were worthwhile. . . ."

He was speaking to Cawley now, afraid of that mature intelligence against which so many party moves and plans had been measured, and often found wanting.

Cawley leaned back in his chair and regarded them. His grating Australian voice, murdered vowels and all, had dignity and conviction.

"Our Labour Party came down", he said quietly, "because of its inadequate economic policy and because we compromised with businessmen and big landowners. When we made moves against exploitation by foreign firms, we aroused God knows what forces with interests external to Australia, but we failed to assess them seriously. We placed a moratorium on uranium mining, while its dangers were explored, but we did not do enough really to carry the people with us.

The businessmen were impatient, and the present government was able to lift the ban.

"Use this tape and I agree that the Government will be forced out of office. I'd like to feel we were ourselves equal to the challenge. What will our position be? Have we thought it through or would we act as pure political opportunists? The Blantyre government has contracted Australia to produce and sell uranium for many years to come. This American contract will have to stand, uranium to be mined, the Aborigines, consequently, to suffer the intrusions of the white man and the loss of their land. Much as we may dislike it, we must never renege on a firm contract of such importance to our only real ally.

"Now, we splash word of this secret wheat-uranium deal of Australia and the United States across the headlines. Who suffers? The Prime Minister, yes. His party, yes. America, yes. Australia, more than anyone. Australia will suffer the odium of having concealed the discovery for the worst of reasons—not to test it thoroughly first, but to get a nice fat safe uranium contract out of its suppression. Since Duquesne is determined to speak, the world must benefit by the discovery being made public. Australia will not lose from Duquesne's announcement—if Blantyre is clever, it may even gain, for Blantyre knows that Australia's image is his political passport."

"My God!" burst out Redneck. "Bloody defeatism! You call yourself a Labour man? What America has done should come out, man! What the Libs have done should be exposed. Would they hesitate to do the same to us if the positions were reversed? My bloody oath they wouldn't. And do you fool yourself America's going to be hurt by this? Was it really hurt by Watergate? No, of course it wasn't. It gained, if anything, because the world is doubly aware now it's a country where abuses—even by the highest in the land—are exposed. And Blantyre will be able to bask in the political benefits of being midwife to the wheat!"

"And I repeat that to seek to be paid in political coin for such an act as this is prostitution," returned Cawley deliberately. "Is that the summit of your ambitions?"

A tense silence followed. Holmes refrained from speaking. Cawley was acting as their safety-valve. None felt proud of the actions whose prizes dangled so enticingly. None wished to have his country's name dragged in the mud by the press of the whole world. But this would happen, and it was a price which had to be paid for power. Power which a Labour government could use wisely. Never again would the party repeat its former leader's disregard of economic realities, but it would return to his social and international visions. It had a role, and the ends justified the means.

Jones spoke for them all. Cawley's loyalty to the party was legendary. He spoke as a rebel in private and he had influenced them all. But never had he gone on record in public against a majority view.

"It is an opportunity we cannot miss," Jones said. "We don't know the outcome. But as a political party our job is to get into power and stay there as long as we can. As Tom said, the Government is so firmly entrenched, only a bomb can dislodge them. We won't get hold of another bomb."

"The trade unions will be with us," contributed O'Donovan.

A decision had been taken without more being said. Holmes rose to his feet and gazed searchingly at them.

"I think it's the right decision." He relaxed, knowing, now, that the outcome had been as inevitable as Australia's endorsement of uranium mining. "Duquesne speaks Monday. He will have ensured, with that press release, that the UN meeting gets real attention by the media. On Tuesday morning—that is, about twelve hours later—I will personally raise the whole affair in open session of Parliament, which is broadcast. By Tuesday night, every living person in Australia will be talking of the Prime Minister's infamous behaviour. A general election will be inevitable."

He paused.

"We'll need to inform party members. I'd like your collaboration in the work we have before us in the next two days. We'll be busy."

His eyes met Cawley's once more and shifted away. He picked up the metal box containing the tape and said: "The tape of the American Ambassador's voice will have to be verified by comparisons with recordings of one of his recent public statements before we use it. Temple is named in it, and we have the reporter Silkin's testimony that he was CIA. We don't know where Temple has got to, and I don't care. The tape will need to be tested in Sydney. We have done this ourselves, but I want independent confirmation. There is a specialised laboratory at Sydney University which the Government itself has used on occasion."

On an impulse Holmes held the box out to Cawley, saying: "Take it to Sydney when you fly back tonight, will you? I'll arrange for the laboratory to contact you."

Cawley's family was in Sydney, and Holmes wanted to demonstrate his sympathy and the liking that he had for him. He put a hand briefly on Cawley's arm as Cawley took the box. Cawley paused, as if to speak, then, after looking impassively at Holmes, he put the box in his briefcase and walked slowly from the room.

That was midday Sunday.

# CHAPTER SEVEN

By Sunday, Duquesne had spent two days working over his statement to the meeting. He had gone to Orvieto, where he booked into a small *pensione.* If Crane had found him by phoning up Rome hotels, so might the Australian Embassy. In Orvieto he felt safe.

Early that morning he was in a state of nerves and headed back to Rome. Just after one o'clock he walked into the Santa Prisca. The boy at the door came forward and said importantly, "Signor Duquesne . . ." and seemed to swell a little with desire to impart information, but before he did more than gesture Duquesne looked past him into the small salon by the entrance. Then he pulled himself up sharply, his shoulder and back neck muscles straining, as Irina rose from a chair to meet him. He stepped back a pace or two and put his clenched hands into his pockets, staring at her speechless.

She said: "Jack." She was dressed—it seemed a crazy choice—in his red sweater, with severely cut grey slacks. Her blonde hair had been cut short and was nearly hidden by a grey tweed cap. She looked a beautiful boyish figure.

Duquesne said, his voice cutting: "I thought I'd left you in Lantao."

Her hand flew to her mouth, and she said again: "Jack." Then she shook her head in a funny little gesture and said: "I must talk to you alone. Please."

He shrugged, and jerked his head in the direction of the stairs.

"You'd better come to my room."

Ignoring the man behind, he led the way up the tiled stairs and into the little sitting room opening off his bedroom. It was to have been their bedroom.

"Your compatriots have caught up with me, then." He made his voice as hard as he could. "Of course. I should have remembered you knew the hotel, where we were both to have stayed. I've even got the double room we ordered. Don't you think it's charming? Sitting room and all."

She recoiled, and her hand went to her mouth again.

"So along comes Irina—complete with sweater, I see. To do what? Open sentimental relations? Charm me back into submission?" He laughed harshly.

"Jack, I can explain." Her eyes were full of pain. Her short hair revealed the well-shaped head which his fingers knew was so beautifully set on that rounded neck, whose skin was so fine, so creamy.

"Oh! Of course you can explain, Irina. The Russians wanted me to work for them, and they used you as the beautiful decoy. It's not an unfamiliar story, I suppose. You were instructed to get to know me. Oh, clever—masterly—the way you picked me up in Canberra. And what a beautifully sustained performance. Right through. Testing me so skilfully to see if I was ripe for"—he paused—"do you call it defection? I was such a *gullible* fool." He was almost sobbing.

"Jack," she faltered. "I *can* explain—"

"No, you can't explain!" he suddenly shouted. "How explain! From beginning to end, trickery. It's filthy and bloody what you did. What you do. Using love . . ."

For a second there was complete silence. The explosion of his anger, grotesque in the pretty little room, had fallen so dead on the unyielding surfaces.

"I wanted to marry you. Well, that's past anyway."

"Jack, I *do* love you." Her voice was hopeless.

"Love. . . ." He attacked the word. "You call that love." He rounded on her suddenly. "Get out."

"Jack, listen." She was white but determined. "It is not what you think. You've finished with me. I understand, Jack. But there *is* a reason why I came. I have a message for you."

"Ah, now we've come to it. What is it this time? Another meeting, I suppose. Another proposition?"

She said: "It's none of my doing. I am a tool, if you can believe that. You're to come with me, now." She went on to say fearfully: "It's your daughter."

"Jane!"

"Yes, your daughter. I have been instructed to tell you that she is in their hands."

His heart went cold.

"What do you mean?" he said very low. He went towards her, looking so crazy she shrank back. "Where is she? She's in Sydney, at school in Sydney."

She made a hopeless gesture.

"I don't *know* anything, only what I was told to tell you. You've got to come with me now. Jack, they mean it. You don't know them. You must come."

Duquesne stared at his watch and went to the telephone. In Australia it would be midnight. Jane was to have spent the day with Meg. She had said so on the phone on Thursday.

"Get me Sydney, Australia. Clovelly 6797106. It's most urgent."

He replaced the receiver and turned to Irina.

She begged, "You are to come with me now and do what they say."

"It's another trick?" While he spoke he knew that what she said was true.

She shook her head, her eyes on his. They stood silently. Then the telephone rang and the operator said: "E interrotto il vostro numero."

"No," he said violently. "Let me talk to Sydney."

"You can talk to Sydney. Go ahead, please."

He was trembling as he said "Yes . . . yes . . . hello!"

An Australian woman's voice said: "The number you want has been disconnected, or else the phone is out of order."

"Disconnected!"

"Yes. It doesn't ring."

He put the receiver down. Irina, standing tall and straight and resolute, said: "You must come. They told me so. It is not for nothing they say so. You can—you *must.*"

The thought that Jane was in danger made him physically ill. He stood fighting for control, thinking of Zubkovich saying, at Casal Palocco: "Your daughter is thirteen, at school in Cremorne, Sydney. Yes, I know. She will visit you when you wish."

He thought of Meg saying to him: "He was a big man, foreign, and he said he was writing an article on wheat. He wanted to know all about your work. How could he have known where I lived?"

Duquesne saw Irina through a veil. Her voice and gestures were unreal. He advanced on her, and his voice cracked as he said: "What do we do?"

"You come with me now. We have to walk, they said. Walk along beside the Palatino. We walk with the traffic going towards the Arch of Constantine. A car will pick us up and take us to the meeting place. We walk next to the road."

"Why the bloody hell can't they come to me?"

Irina said: "They don't know where you are. I said I would tell them if I could see you alone, first. Jack, how could I not do it?"

"Get going." He threw open the door and motioned her through.

Irina's eyes brimmed. Then without a word she preceded him out and down the stairs. The porter was standing at the door. He hastened to open the inner white-painted hall-door, and as they went through Irina's eyes met his. The porter nodded very slightly and said: "Your taxi is still waiting."

He went out afterwards and watched them walk down the drive to the car, and then he took a paper from his pocket and went to the telephone. He dialled a local number and smiled as he said into the receiver: "Si, sono usciti in questo momento. He and the young lady. She is with him, yes. And he wears a red sweater. A red sweater and grey pants. Also he wears sunglasses and a cap."

The line went dead. The porter looked at the receiver stupidly for a moment and then returned to his seat in the hall. She was a *signorina molto bella,* the *straniera,* obviously full of practical jokes. He picked up his newspaper again and settled down. Perhaps she would move in with Duquesne now. He had a double room. *Beato lui.* Crazy, though, this girl. Ten thousand lire she'd given him, just to make a phone call and give that misleading description. He wouldn't mind having her stay in the hotel. These foreigners. They threw their money around, some of them, as long as they were not French.

Outside they climbed into the waiting taxi, and Irina said to the driver: "To the Colosseo, along the Via di San Gregorio. Just before the Colosseo. I will tell you."

Beside her, Duquesne was prey to a vast helplessness and horror. If they had Jane, if they hurt Jane . . . The old faded palazzi of the Aventine Hill slid by on either side, and he saw only Jane's tight face, taken to extremes of shame that she might break and cry in front of strangers, set and terrified, Jane's eyes, bright blue, bright with agony.

Stopped at the traffic lights in the Piazza di Porta Capena, the foul suspended heat of a hundred petrol-exhausts, the raucous grind of the panting vehicles around them were part of the agony of not knowing about Jane, not being with Jane. From the Viale delle Terme di Caracalla people were spilling out over the road. Placards held high bore the red hammer and sickle, and others said "No alla violenza" and "Vota Comunista."

The taxi thrust its way into the Via di San Gregorio. Irina told the driver to stop. They were climbing out, and she was paying him off. Down the road they left the demonstrators behind, and the people thinned and became Sunday *passeggiata,* little knots of bewildered tourists mingling with the touts and thieves and itinerant vendors who now dominated so many parts of the decadent old city.

Duquesne saw it all as in a nightmare. They began walking.

"I'll go ahead of you. Keep well behind me, not close."

Irina's eyes were bright now and reckless. Duquesne understood nothing. She stood a moment looking intently at him, and then her mouth trembled. She made a half-salute, turned and began walking along the footpath, close to the road. She stopped once and drew some dark glasses from her pocket and put them on. After she had got a little way ahead he began walking, too.

He kept his eyes on Irina. Her sweater and the loose grey slacks hid the shape of her figure. She walked with a long stride, slowly, in thick-soled flat shoes. With her broad shoulders, her cap, her femininity seemed hidden. His eyes registered these facts, but his mind and senses, strained towards Jane, did not. He waited for the car that would pull up beside him soon. It would crawl slowly along, letting others by.

From further back came the orchestrated shouting of the demonstrators. A bus ground past, forerunner of another surge of traffic released from the lights back at the piazza. A silly tricar affair passed, propelled by bicycle and containing two youths and a girl. And at that moment someone screamed, and Duquesne saw Irina stop, stand for a second in an odd suspended attitude as though she had dropped something, and then she slid down upon the pavement. He heard shouts and cries against the roar of traffic.

A woman coming towards him started running, clumsily. He saw her perfect teeth as she opened her mouth to scream "Stanno tirando! They're firing!" He thought he heard the quick swish of bullets, and others began running, they were not sure where.

When he got to Irina she lay on the ground on her back, her head twisted to one side. Just above the broad cheekbone, through the temple, was a neat round hole. It was like the smut she had had on her face in Lantao. He was kneeling beside her pleading and swearing. But even before he pulled up the sweater to place a hand on her heart he knew she was dead.

Just before the crowd, still frightened but now excited, closed in, he pushed himself through it, leaving Irina to the mercy of the Roman mob.

Up above the road, on the Palatine Hill, in the thick cover of acanthus and fennel on the closed-off side, where not even lovers ventured, the marksman waited a few seconds after the red sweater crumpled before rapidly and expertly placing a few more bullets on the ground close to dispersed knots of people. It was to be hoped the uncontrollable ricochets would not hurt anyone. He had expected not trippers by now but demonstrators, whom he would have enjoyed scaring. But, like all things Italian, the march was late. But soon these people would have discipline taught them.

He put the rifle out of sight amongst the acanthus which had given him such excellent cover. It was a pity to discard such a superbly accurate example of precision engineering. But the newspapers would learn that it was an American rifle.

He rested his eyes, tired from long concentration, on the glowing clustered roofs and walls and churches of the Coelian Hill, floating in golden brown isolation between road and sky, and on the Colosseum far over to the left, gleaming pinkish white and innocent now in the soft afternoon air.

Before turning to thread his way swiftly up the bank through the towering stone-pines to the small green olive-planted *esedra* above, he patted the pocket which held his little radio, and looked carefully round to make sure he had left nothing behind which might be traced to him. He picked up and pocketed the paper from a bar of chocolate and the skin of a banana which he had consumed while waiting. He had had to wait a long time, up there on the hill.

# CHAPTER EIGHT

HE COULD NOT HAVE LEFT HER except for Jane. But he couldn't become involved as a witness. He found himself walking, shoulder muscles knotted, his nails biting into his palms, making pain for himself. Because the demonstrators blocked the way behind, he went towards the Colosseum. Through a haze he saw the traffic was thinning. At the Colosseum were police coaches, full of men, their helmets glinting, the visors pushed up.

Horror invested the scene. He thought he saw it through wave after wave of red-tinged gauze and wondered if he would faint. A part of him was sobbing. He could only walk, and presently he juggled his assorted raw thoughts and feelings, like pictures stuck to his brain, inside his head, and detached Jane from the rest, concentrating. He must ring through to Australia, and the only way was to go back to the Santa Prisca because he did not know where else he could phone. Should he make contact with the police in Sydney?

Sirens screamed and wailed, and a police car shot by. An ambulance followed. It must be for Irina. Another police car. Most people, hardened to such sights, did not bother to turn their heads.

Somewhere beyond the Colosseum he found a taxi and directed the driver to the Santa Prisca. The man looked at him curiously. Duquesne did not realise that his face was drained of all colour. He should not have left Irina. But he couldn't think both of her and of Jane. And Jane was somewhere, needing him. For Irina there was nothing to be done.

At the hotel the doorman had disappeared. It was five o'clock. Sitting on the side of his bed Duquesne gave the operator the number of Jane's school. While he waited he drank a large glass of whisky, which steadied him a little. He was lucky to have the call go through almost at once. He could hear the phone ring and ring at the other end. On and on it went. Finally, almost at screaming point, he heard a man's voice say: "Yes, yes. What is it? Hello?"

"I want to talk to Jane Duquesne."

"Jane Duquesne," repeated the man stupidly. "Where would she be?"

"Isn't that Bexley House School?" asked Duquesne fearfully.

"Yes. It's the middle of the night, too," said the man. He had a very Australian voice.

"I'm speaking from Italy. I'm her father. It's terribly urgent. An emergency. For God's sake wake her up and bring her to the phone. I have to speak to her." He could hear his voice rising.

The man agreed, grumbling. They were all asleep. He'd have to wake the matron. There was a long, long wait, with the operator breaking in now and then to ask him if he was still connected.

Duquesne knew they were the longest minutes he had ever passed. He wanted to scream with anguish when the man's voice said again: "Yes? Mr. Duquesne?"

"Is she there?"

"She's coming on the line now."

Standing hunched over the receiver, Duquesne heard: "Daddy! They said it's you. Is it Daddy?"

"Jane." He fought to control himself, the tears raining down his face.

"What's wrong?" Her voice, sleepy at first, was very small and frightened now, and it jerked him into calmness.

"Jane, are you all right? Were you asleep?"

"Oh, Daddy, of course. Sound. We all are. Isn't it the middle of the night? Are you still in Italy?"

"Yes."

"Oh, Daddy, have you seen the Pope? He was on TV here. And he spoke English. I thought he would speak Latin."

"Not yet, I haven't seen him. Jane, are you all right? Everything going well?"

"Of course, Daddy." Her voice was puzzled. "Why?"

"Oh, nothing. Is Mummy OK?"

"Yes. I saw her today again. She brought me back in time for tea."

"Were you out all day?"

"Yes. At Gran's. Daddy, guess what?" Jane was waking up now. "Troy's had puppies."

She launched into a long description, and Duquesne sat listening, weak with relief, breathing into his answers what love and longing he could convey over all those thousands of miles, pretending to joke, talking on and on, regardless, until Jane said: "We've been talking twenty minutes. There's a clock here."

Lightheaded, he sat there for a long time trying to collect his faculties. At last he picked up the telephone and asked them to try Meg's number again. After a long wait the operator in Australia said, surprisingly: "You're through. Go ahead, please."

Meg was also sleepy but, he could tell, overjoyed to hear him. Words tumbled out of her. She had read the newspaper report. She was full of questions. And support.

He sketched in as much of his situation as he safely could for her, then asked about her telephone. There had been a silly accident, she said. A telephone company mechanic had been in that morning—just before she went out for the day—checking on all the phones in the building, he had said. When she got back that night the phone was dead. Only later had she discovered the mechanic had pulled out the wires and not connected them up again. Terribly careless of him.

Though loath to alarm her, he told Meg why he was calling. Then he rang off, knowing she would do whatever possible to protect Jane. She promised to see the headmistress the first thing in the morning.

Duquesne decided to sleep elsewhere that night. Irina could have lied when she said only she knew his hotel. Or someone could have followed her. Until the meeting was over he would not be safe. Hastily he changed into his good suit, packed a shirt and essentials into his briefcase and called a taxi. He left the rest of his luggage in his room.

When the taxi came he told the driver to take him to the Quirinale. He was lucky. They had just had a cancellation. On an impulse he produced his Gleason passport. In his room he showered, and sat down to think.

Jane was safe. The Russians had been bluffing. But he was inclined to think they had tampered with Meg's phone, anticipating his call to her. Using Irina, they had positioned him in the Via di San Gregorio for a bullet. To kill him. The car had not come. The bullet which killed Irina was certainly meant for him. Wasn't it? There had been other bullets. He did not think anyone else had been hit. Were they all random shots into the crowd by the Red Brigade or some other terrorist group? No—random shooting into a crowd didn't make much sense. And those weren't random shots, because no one else had been hit. But to make it seem like a terrorist episode was safer for them. There was always a risk when you shot someone. It was better in the open, with a chance for the gunman to get away. Only they had shot Irina instead. Could they have done it as a warning to him? Because her usefulness to them was over now and it was safer for them? Because they thought she might be about to desert them and join him?

He would stay in his hotel this time until the meeting. Until the meeting was over he was in danger. They were out to get him because of the newspaper report. He pulled it from his briefcase and read it again:

ANOTHER GREEN REVOLUTION? FIREWORKS LIKELY AT UN CONFERENCE

Startling facts concerning governmental constraints on plant breeding and its exploitation were alleged by leading Australian plant scientist Dr. Jack Duquesne in Rome yesterday during an interview with our Rome correspondent.

The work of plant breeders is of vital importance in a world which—by the year 2000—will need almost twice as much food as it does now. Already there are half a billion underfed people in the world. The battle against hunger is also a race against time.

It is expected that, at a United Nations meeting which opens at the Food and Agriculture Organisation headquarters on 2 June 1980, Dr. Duquesne will throw down the gauntlet for making full use of the work of plant breeders. Your correspondent understands that he will cite chapter and verse in exposing instances of political manoeuvring by major powers against the interests of the world's hungry.

Dr. Duquesne hinted that he would himself be giving details at the UN meeting of an immensely important breakthrough in reaching higher plant yields, a breakthrough suppressed up till now as a result of political pressures by three powerful countries.

It was an article to strike fear into official breasts. Any one of the three countries might wish him safely out of the way. He thought also of Zubkovich and the personal grudge he must bear him.

He pulled from his bag his address to the meeting, and tried to read it over. But he saw only Irina's twisted form and staring eyes, the neat bullet-hole and the trickle of blood.

Death was horribly final. Furiously angry and hurt as he had been recently, he had never really stopped loving the Irina he used to know.

He had to wait for the 2240 news on television Channel One for the afternoon's demonstration and the pictures of a stretcher being put into an ambulance. The body, he knew, was Irina's. She was described as a beautiful foreign tourist who had been caught by a stray bullet. A madman's stray bullet, or was the shooting the work of the Brigate Rosse? The police had as yet no statement to make. *Indagini* were proceeding.

Duquesne watched the news through, then he took a sleeping pill, left a call for 7.30, and the horror of the day was finally snuffed out.

# CHAPTER NINE

He ordered two morning papers with his breakfast. An Irina who was just recognisable stared sightlessly from a blurred police photograph in *Tempo. Messaggero* did better with an old-fashioned artist's illustration of the killing. Irina had both arms flung high and a look of anguish as the bullet sped towards her, but she was beautiful.

The United Nations meeting began at ten. At nine Duquesne phoned the secretary and was told where to pick up the documentation. At 9.30 he ordered a taxi and at 9.35 went out into the Via Nazionale, by now in the grip of its daily avalanche of vehicles, and was borne up to Santa Maria Maggiore and by circuitous back routes over the Colle Oppio to the white mass of the Food and Agriculture Organisation.

He wanted to arrive approximately twenty minutes late. The name-badge had been sent to all participants when they had accepted invitations. He directed the taxi to the side-entrance of the FAO building. The doorman looked at his badge in silence, and Duquesne walked to one of the less-used corner lifts which took him near a bridge connecting the main building with the conference building, thus completely avoiding the main doors. He looked at the slightly flickering announcement-screen: "UN/FAO ad hoc meeting on grain production." That would be his meeting. It was being held in the Red Room. He smiled to himself. He thought that its companion conference-room, the Green Room, would have been more appropriate.

He registered at the table of an uninterested secretary and collected his papers at the documents-desk without encountering anyone he knew. From the red signal-lamp in the corridor he knew that the conference was already in session. It must just have begun, after the customary quarter of an hour of delay. As he presented his pass at the door a man he vaguely knew pressed forward, but Duquesne shook his head brusquely and brushed past him.

A pretty messenger girl—she looked the age when she should still be at school—was by his side in a moment.

"Dr. Duquesne? I'll take you to your place."

The Red Room he knew well—a spacious square room intended for meetings of one to two hundred people. It was panelled in a polished wood of mid-brown with fine grain. One whole side was window, looking out in the direction of the Colosseum.

Duquesne hastily looked towards the raised dais where the director-general of the FAO and someone whom he correctly supposed was an under-secretary of the UN flanked the chairman. Grey-haired, impeccably dressed, his impatience to get on with the job just barely contained by the formal requirements of his office, the chairman was a famous plant scientist and a recent Nobel Prizewinner. It was he who more than any other single man had inspired and fought for the developments which had collectively become known in the late 1960s as the Green Revolution. Duquesne respected him immensely.

The little messenger girl had scarcely smiled her appreciation at Duquesne's "Grazie" as he slid into his place near the middle and three rows from the front, when his shoulder was tapped from behind.

"Dr. Duquesne. I am Clive Trevor, agricultural attaché at the embassy." There was no need for him to say which embassy. Duquesne had grown up with that twangy, slightly insincere accent. "The Ambassador has asked—"

"Go to hell!" snapped Duquesne, loud enough for Austria and Bangladesh on either side of him to stare.

The Australian diplomat wavered, uncertain. His job did not include accepting that behaviour, but on the other hand the Ambassador had been adamant. The girl in the Ambassador's outer office, who was one of the attaché's tennis group, had whispered that the Prime Minister himself had been on the phone to them three times in the last twenty-four hours. The Australian diplomat pushed a sealed envelope towards Duquesne: "I was asked to give you this."

Duquesne ignored the proffered envelope and turned to greet Bangladesh. The Australian retired, hating the constrictions of his job.

"Gentlemen—oh, I beg your pardon—ladies and gentlemen"—and the chairman indicated his apologies to an impassive Egyptian lady—"our agenda is straightforward. This meeting is meant not so much for decisions as for discussions which will lead to decisions elsewhere. It is a meeting to appraise the present situation and the prospects as we see them for food grain production in the developing countries. I was privileged to play a part in getting the Green Revolution started. As we all know, the momentum engendered then has ceased. Now we must face the question: How can we get the Green Revolution rolling again?

"Our meeting arrangements are simple. I shall first ask the Director-General of the FAO and then the Under-Secretary of the UN to tell us how their organisations see the problem. Then we will hear from each of the experts whom we have invited to attend in their personal capacities to appraise the problem. This will take all today.

"Tomorrow morning, I shall give you my synthesis of their views. Then we will hear from the government representatives. The majority of countries, I am glad to see, are represented here." And he nodded to the well-filled chamber. "Now I give the floor to the Director-General of the FAO."

The Director-General tapped his microphone, and the light at the base came on. He began to speak in French, and there was a rush of clicks as the predominantly English-speaking audience tried to find this interpretation for their headsets.

Duquesne listened as the speaker outlined the problem of loss of growth in yields of grains. A clear and authoritative presentation, and Duquesne was following it with interest when the same messenger girl approached unseen and began to whisper in his ear. For several moments Duquesne understood nothing. The girl's lips were so close to his ear he thought he felt their smooth touch. For a split second Irina caressed his ear with quick little flicks of her tongue and the meeting was only a hollow shell around him.

"Pardon. What did you say?" he asked the messenger girl.

"The Australian Ambassador has sent a message. He says that before your statement to the conference he must speak to you. He is waiting for you in the office of the Deputy Director-General. I will take you there."

Duquesne thought rapidly, half-hearing the words of the Director-General, who was urging that the effectiveness of scientific effort be judged by how production did actually improve.

"The man with dirt under his nails, accepted by the farmer of Asia or Africa, is more valuable in our time than the writer of smooth scientific articles in learned periodicals on the minutiae of his subject even though the man with dirty nails remains unknown and with an inferior income. . . ."

Duquesne noted his agreement even while he considered the message given him. Hell, what was there to lose?

"Tell the Ambassador that I consider attendance at this meeting more important than talking to him," he said.

The girl looked startled. Like all Latins, she still had an exaggerated respect for rank. She said: "Please, could you write this?"

Duquesne wrote the message as bluntly as he had said it. His damned country was becoming ridiculously exigent. Why should he come running just because an ambassador had crooked his little finger?

He ceased to pay attention to the speeches while he reviewed once again what he would say. He would blend two themes. One would deal with the world situation, which, God knew, still presented the paradox of famine amongst plenty. Imports of cereals by poor countries were mounting steadily, and it was only a matter of time before any deliveries not prefaced by payment in a convertible currency or some political IOU would cease. The other theme would then weigh in with his Australian experience of what appeared to be a major breakthrough, but one that had been suppressed in the interests of Australia and the United States. The bite of his address would be the contrast between the two themes, the insolent and cynical disregard in rich countries like his own for inconvenient discoveries, no matter what they presaged for welfare in poor countries, and the desperate need for higher food-crop productivity in poor countries.

The Under-Secretary from the United Nations, who had been speaking, finished talking. Duquesne realised he had really heard next to nothing of his speech. There was a brief pause while the chairman leaned back and talked earnestly to three men who had mounted the dais during the speech. There was a general nodding of heads, and the three men withdrew to the back of the podium.

Now, if speakers were taken alphabetically, it would be his turn, Duquesne thought. El Ghamani from Egypt, Herriot from France. No, he was first in the list of invited experts.

The chairman raised his voice.

"I have two announcements."

Duquesne stiffened. What was happening?

"First, the Commission of the European Communities, better known as the Common Market, has asked that a speaker from their secretariat be permitted to intervene as an independent expert. I will rule immediately that this request is out of order. The essence of the status of an independent expert in our meeting is that he does not represent a national or supranational authority."

The spokesman for the Commission began to raise his arm to ask for the floor, to point out the erroneous representation by the chairman of the request by the Commission. Then he felt the surge of annoyance or hostility to the Brussels bureaucracy of many of those in the room, and quickly changed his mind.

"My second announcement is of a very different order. I believe that it will startle this meeting." The chairman paused, not so much for effect as for his own emotion. "I will read the communication which has been passed to me. I shall read it slowly because there has been no opportunity to get copies to the interpreters and it is vital that it be interpreted correctly. The announcement reads:

" 'The governments of Australia, the Union of Soviet Socialist Republics and the United States of America take the present occasion to announce to the scientific world a fundamental breakthrough in wheat breeding and the establishment of a permanent tripartite organisation of the three countries to test, to develop and—if it proves successful—to assist materially in the exploitation of the new wheat by developing countries. The three governments have agreed to endow the tripartite organisation with an initial fund of two hundred million dollars, and for the following ten years each will subscribe twenty-five million dollars a year in inflation-indexed funds. It will thus become a major new organisation in the fight against poverty and hunger.

" 'The breakthrough in question is the discovery by the Commonwealth Scientific and Industrial Research Organisation of Australia of a variety of wheat which in ways that cannot at present be explained has acquired the ability to grow and to yield far above any comparable food grain in tropical conditions. . . .' "

Duquesne sat stunned. What was happening? How could these countries be announcing his discovery and promising to develop it? He knew firsthand that two of the countries had decided to suppress it, and he had just rejected the efforts of the third to get hold of both him and the wheat. And what could he say to the meeting now? The paper he was to read in a few minutes wove scientific reporting and assessment with details of the unfolding of an Australian official policy which as of this very moment no longer existed. He had been outwitted again. The loner could not beat the armies.

Then he heard his name. The chairman was continuing to read.

" '. . . whom we all know played a major role in this discovery. Were it not for the enthusiasm of Dr. Jack Duquesne and that flair which a true scientist displays, not just for recognising visible evidence of the unusual but also for intuitively knowing when this represents great potential, then indeed the discovery would never have been made.

" 'The governments of the three countries, in recognition of his scientific contribution and knowing his excellent record in a number of developing countries, offer the post of director of the tripartite organisation to Dr. Jack Duquesne. In order that he could prepare his assessment paper for this present conference uninfluenced by the role which he may in future discharge, the offer of this post, which was decided some time ago, is made known to Dr. Duquesne only now.' " The chairman paused. "Indeed, at this very instant."

A delegate in the rear began to clap, and the clapping swelled. Duquesne endeavoured to think. Had he won after all? Had his threatened disclosures forced the hands of the three governments? Was there a catch? Of course it was an agreement reached only now and in the greatest haste. This was the message the Australian diplomat had tried to get to him; this was why the Ambassador had wanted to see him. But they had been clever. What had the announcement said? ". . . In order that he could prepare his assessment paper . . . uninfluenced. . . ." If he made public what was at present in his paper scheduled to be read this morning, he could not accept the post. If he accepted the post, he could not subsequently reveal what the countries had tried to do. Every man has his price. Was this his price?

As the clapping flickered out, the chairman glanced at a note which had just been handed to him and said: "I will give the floor to Dr. Duquesne. The three governments are sure that he will wish to react now, at least in principle, to their offer. Dr. Duquesne?"

Duquesne slowly pressed the white button on the base of his mike. The round fine mesh of the mike stared at him. Silence became absolute in the conference-room.

"Mr. Chairman," said Duquesne. "I am honoured to accept this post, which will enable me . . ."

But his words were then drowned in vigorously renewed clapping.

Back in his hotel that night, Duquesne, disregarding expense, spent the evening in telephone calls to Australia. He spoke lastly to Silkin.

"What happened?" he demanded. "Woods was so noncommittal."

"Misfired, I'm afraid. The evidence—er—disappeared."

"No. How?"

"Cawley split on his chief. He didn't approve of the plan and he took the story to the PM on Sunday night."

Duquesne was dumbfounded.

"But . . ."

"The PM jumped the gun in the only way he could. It culminated in the offer to you."

"Good God." Duquesne was filled with wonder. "What possessed Cawley?"

"The honour of his party and his country, he told Holmes. I should say also age."

"More likely age."

"And the arrogance to act alone and humility in meeting the cost," said Silkin, his deep voice getting deeper.

"Well, yes, it took courage."

"*You'd* know."

"I'm not, however, a politician. I guess that's the end of him."

"The air was getting pretty blue in party headquarters, Holmes said. Redneck described him as a diseased rat he wouldn't pursue into a sewer. The other epithets were rather less wholesome."

Duquesne laughed, and Silkin said, with a note of envy: "You got what you wanted."

Duquesne, prisoner of so many conflicting emotions, said simply: "Taking stock is impossible at the moment."

And meant it.

# CHAPTER TEN

FOUR DAYS LATER, on a bright day of early summer, a handful of people stood at Irina's graveside among the old dusty cypresses, giants rearing to the sky above the crowded monuments of the cemetery.

Vasily Sanin stood big and black-clothed and in the grip of a passionate grief and hatred. Hatred of Duquesne, who met his eyes and almost physically recoiled at what he saw there. So Vasily, too, had loved her.

A middle-aged man called Colonel Eaton, summoned post-haste to Rome from Canberra two weeks before, also avoided Vasily's eyes, avoided everyone's eyes. He stood beside a seamed and broken, thin old man, who had arrived just too late to see his daughter alive. Her father had thought Irina would have liked to be buried in Rome, a city she had loved, where she and her mother had spent four years together in Irina's teens. Close by was her mother's grave.

"In blessed sleep give eternal rest, O Lord, to your deceased servants, and confer on them eternal memory," intoned the priest.

A lorry ground past outside in the street. The old man sobbed as the dark-coped priest's sad sung recital continued gently. He was grateful to feel the Colonel's hand solid and strong under his arm, to feel that big solid body beside him. The Colonel had been so good. Ivan Grigoriev was grateful, though bewildered. The Colonel, a total stranger, had taken him into his own apartment, had shown unceasing kindness from the moment Ivan Grigoriev had turned up at the Embassy. But why? The old man never stopped asking why. Why had Irina been in Rome, why had she—of all the people in the Via di San Gregorio that afternoon—been the one to get a bullet? Why, why . . . oh God. Why? Irina, his darling, his beautiful one. But the Colonel was so good. . . .

Colonel Eaton had not told him why. He was thinking now of Irina's first visit to him in Canberra, when she had revealed she was under pressure from the Russians. Because of her father, who had wanted to see his daughter and also his brother once more before he died, who had been detained at the frontier when leaving Russia because he was carrying the manuscript of a friend. Subversive literature. He had been taken to prison immediately.

In Canberra the Russians had promised her her father's release. The price? She was to carry out a specific task for them. She was to watch Duquesne and report to them; to get for them, if she could, samples of the wheat; to gain his confidence and affection.

Irina had gone to Australian intelligence. Colonel Eaton had had to go carefully. The girl could have been lying. But they had checked her story very carefully, and there was no doubt the father was a prisoner. They had set Irina to report to them as well. It seemed an approach would be made to Duquesne by the Russians, and very likely through her.

She had played both sides, of course—passed information to the Russians, but information of small value, carefully selected by the Australian authorities. She had told Eaton of Duquesne's intention to leave Australia, it was true, but begged Eaton to pick him up only on departure from Sydney, as otherwise the Russians would realise she was playing them false. It had not been her fault if someone had slipped up—somewhere along the line—and the pair had got through the immigration check at Sydney that day. Two men had lost their jobs, but the Colonel's face reddened still to think of the gross carelessness.

The Colonel was thinking also of Irina's visit to him the afternoon before her death, when she had cried: "Don't you see what they plan? I'm to lead him to his death, I'm sure of it. It's a trap. If I don't do this, my father stays in Russia. They've told me so. He's so old. Seventy-three. Do something! *You* can! Save Jack!"

She had not been convinced, either, when he had said: "Yes. Try not to get upset. We'll have to see what can be done."

Almost fatherly, his manner. Fatherly!

The Colonel's lips pressed together, and his chin went out. He had his job to do, and his job had been to do nothing. He could not have known, could he—or should he have known?—that the girl would take matters into her own hands and fool the marksman by dressing to her own description of Duquesne's appearance? Who could mistake that red sweater? Duquesne's sweater, so the word had reached his embassy. It was obvious she had done so. What a business. A bad business. Hardest thing he'd ever had to do, resist her plea. Those eyes of hers, boring into him, seeing right through him.

Well, Duquesne was safe now and one job less for the Colonel's outfit. The Colonel looked across at him. The world before him. And, if things had gone differently, Duquesne would have been down there now in the coffin instead of Irina.

The Agricultural Attaché, forced for some days now into proximity with Duquesne, was also looking at Duquesne surreptitiously. Duquesne. A transformation. His fortunes gloriously restored. The man whom everyone wanted to consult, to interview. People were apt to materialise about him where he walked, and a faint excitement hung in the air. Duquesne looked different, too. He seemed to have grown a new smooth skin all over. He had status, the aura of success and the power of patronage which the disposal of large government funds gives to those with authority to open the tap. And he had the assurance of a man who had the power to accomplish an aim that he believed in completely and passionately.

And only a week before—God, that night in the Embassy. The frantic scene, with Duquesne disappeared into thin air, the telephone calls back and forth the entire night, calls between ambassadors, between heads of state, and in Canberra, on a line kept open between the Lodge and the Rome Embassy, the Prime Minister cursing their heads off.

The Attaché looked at Duquesne, his dislike mingled with respect. He had had the premiers of three countries hanging on his words. And now—Duquesne had it made.

The priest had finished his recital. The coffin was lowered into the grave. Irina's father made a blind and piteous gesture with his hands, as though he would arrest her burial. And then the mourners each took a handful of earth and threw it on the coffin.

To Duquesne, standing there watching the grave filled in, Irina spoke and laughed, regarding him across many shared hours. And she nestled her head again into his shoulder through long nights, and said again, at Sydney Airport: "Jack, with all my heart, I want things to be well for you. With all my heart."

And once again revolt rose in him, flooding through his heart and his loins. And he wanted to try to stay her going, to throw himself upon her grave. And he wanted to beg forgiveness, though for exactly what he did not know.

Getting into the new Mercedes afterwards, Duquesne said to the embassy official in a strained voice: "That tall man you spoke to . . . Colonel someone. . . ."

"He's from Canberra." The other's eyes were fixed firmly on something the other side of the window. He had been seconded for some days past to assist Duquesne—an unwelcome task.

"And the old man?" asked Duquesne.

"Her father. The Russians permitted him to leave."

"Her father! I must speak to him." Duquesne reached forward to tell the driver.

The other man looked at him with dislike.

"The old man is quite enough upset," he said, and then added deliberately: "Even without knowing of the self-sacrifice of his daughter—for you even more than for him."

"Self-sacrifice?"

Grief and affront gave way to clarity. And suddenly the pieces formed a pattern. Duquesne was again in the street where Irina had been killed. And she was there walking ahead of him and wearing that unmistakable red sweater of his. Offering her body in place of his to the bullets of a hidden marksman. His anger at her earlier deception gave way to a desolation he would know many times in the years ahead. He sat frozen.

"You're due in a few minutes to address the developing countries," his companion said. "It's a critical meeting to get action started."

Duquesne drew a deep breath.

"Yes," he said. "Yes." He forced himself to sit upright. "Tell the driver to hurry. We mustn't be late."

The Mercedes continued on its way.